Also by Charles S. Whistler

Beyond Certainty, 2008

A Humanist's Introduction to God, 2011

The Baby on the Doorstep, 2014

The Mighty Unconquerable, 2015

Artists and Models

Charles Whistler

authorHOUSE®

AuthorHouse™
1663 Liberty Drive
Bloomington, IN 47403
www.authorhouse.com
Phone: 1 (800) 839-8640

Published by AuthorHouse 11/26/2018

ISBN: 978-1-5462-6261-9 (sc)
ISBN: 978-1-5462-6260-2 (e)

Print information available on the last page.

For

Dee and RPN

CONTENTS

PREPARATION

A glint of the sun
After the rain
Lasts a blink of a second!
Catch it quickly!
It is gone!

Don't waste your life!
Nothing is as vital
As a raindrop!
Catch it!
Quickly, quickly!

That new leaf
Is squeaking to unfurl—
Quickly, quickly--
Those squeaks are for you--

Quickly, quickly
Don't delay--
Clouds are about to cloak the sun!
Quickly, quickly!

Quickly, quickly
As completely as you can
Capture what can't be captured—
Repetition is mere illusion--
Return is mere deception—

*

At once—
Look at the bougainvillea—
You will never see it again
With the same majesty—

*

The first bite
Never can be duplicated--

*

Towers of every height
Now now now
Catching the brilliance
Of the rising sun—

*

LIGHT MORE PRECIOUS THAN GOLD

A sky of sunshine
Is worth more
Than all the world's gold—
A ray of moonlight
Is worth more
Than a night of sleep--
A field of grass
An icicle melting
Is the wealth of nations

And our lives—
This moment—

*

Inside four walls
While all that sun is shining?
How irresistible
Must a gift be?

*

The sun beats upon the philodendron
And turns it into gold—
The sun sinks into the bronze faun
And sets its heart to beating--
Miracles are ever flourishing—
We capture so few of them--

*

On this perfect summer afternoon
I will live among the light
Forever—
You say there is no forever?
Forever is as long as we can take it—

*

Sunshine expected—

When it doesn't come
How welcome
The shade—

*

Fortunate people
Share the warmth of the sun
With fortunate people—

*

Sunlight makes beautiful
All who catch it—

*

A sky so intensely blue
Everything is dissolved in it--
Instantly
We're about to disappear—

*

This clear day--
At a certain point
Everything is invisible
In itself—

*

My mind
Is blowing out the window
With a breeze beside itself
And the green of spring—

*

The earth sprouts mountains
As easily as blades of grass—
The earth raises derricks and cranes
As easily as it does daffodils--
The earth propels airplanes
As easily as it does bubbles
In champagne in slender tulips—
The earth coordinates error
As grand strategy
And the wildest leaps of theory
As easily as it does
Temperatures racing around the world--
Easy, easy—
Creation
Easy, easy—

*

BE SURPRISED

The world comes to our doorstep
And sees locked windows and doors—

Open them up—

The world knocks
At our door--
Don't wonder who it is--
Open—

*

Life always
Is in-between moments—
(No wonder life tends to the absurd)
Plans never go as they're supposed to—
We dignify life
By giving it purpose as if it were so--
If it weren't, how would we survive?
We discard its in-betweenness
And lose time to live—

*

Wherever you choose to live
Make sure you can see sky—

*

The sun, with its shadows
Flowing smoothly

Over sand
Over gravel
Over mountains
Over worlds—
We forget
All the other interventions--

*

So rewarding
So utterly humbling
The world of beauty
Spread before us—
We might commit
To letting nothing
But bare feet
Touch it—

*

Of course we should know
All the world was created
Just for us
As it was
For all those millions before us—

*

Beauty is uncalculated—

It grows spontaneously
Out of nowhere—
Most of it is received
Without thought
And prior experience—
It is as if it were always part of us
And is now newly discovered--
Sometimes we polish it—
Rough edges can accompany it
But more beauty is discovered
To be beauty
When we do nothing to it—
We pretend to work it over
But mostly it is
What is done to us—

*

If beauty is your guiding light
You're following the wrong signal—

*

Who gave us the idea
That asking for modest gifts
Made us more worthy?
We don't have to belittle ourselves--
We've been given more
Than we can ever use—

Expect more
And reward will be found—

*

We have grandeur within us—
We must be wary of anyone
Who tries to tell us differenty—

*

We attempt to capture
So many lights and sounds
Of a glorious universe
That often we miss the glory
Within us--

*

Let a little bit of you
Into your life—

*

Beauty is a safety valve
Giving breathing space
To endless life—

*

We draw from miracles
And take so much in—
Part of our miracle is
That we exhale so much more—

*

Living in the instant means
Living in beauty—
Everything is beautiful--
What is perceived as totality
Is instant beauty
Is instant truth—
No positive
No negative
No conclusion
No beginning
No end
No names
No god—
We are blessed
In our sainthood—

*

The "perfect" man is he
Whose every thought
Of every act and color asks
How it affects him—
If it doesn't, he drops it—

If it affects him lightly
He gives it little concern
If it's another time or place
He gives little time to it—
If he's the "perfect" man
He doesn't give himself over to others—
His thought and action involves
Only himself—
Who suggests perfection is a good thing?

*

To see with clarity and objectivity
We first must master "stillness—"
Stillness is a word so upside down
In definition
That it is close to useless—
Stillness has no positive-negative
connection
No big or little impact
No outside sources—
Those are captured from other powers
Meant with varying incentive
To sway or control us—
Little things can enchain us
Little things can last a lifetime—
(Don't be fooled!
Every distraction is meant to control us--)
Without positive-negative concern
We act from inner purpose

Find our individual purpose
And achieve stillness—

*

Nature does nothing for beauty's sake—
Beauty is an unintentional part of
creation—
God has no such thought in mind—
It is for us to discover it everywhere—
When mind came beauty came—

*

When we need not make
Comparisons
When all is beautiful
And let's say heartfelt
What's the difference between a gift
Costing hundreds of dollars
And a gift conceived in heart beats?

*

I dropped something behind me
That looked like gold—
No doubt it truly was—
I dropped a coin of gold—
Who cares its value?
It was mine—

I don't know how I acquired it—
Did you bother to pick it up?
It was gold, wasn't it?
What value could we give it?

*

If it were turned over
That dull plastic lid on the sidewalk
Would prove to be solid gold—
Solid gold!
No need to move it—
All the world is beyond comparison—
The world needs us to find
Only a new understanding--

*

What a marvel—
An atom the weight of a universe—
Everyone is told
An idea is the universe's weight
A baker's dozen of universes
And even lighter than a light
Blazing or extinguished—

*

Our intelligence
Little or great

Adapts to mistakes
It seldom recognizes—

*

We so fix the idea of size
In the young
They think it's of monstrous importance
The rest of their lives—

*

"Big" escapes being seen
By being so much of the scene—
The obvious is already hidden--
The obvious is the trickiest to find—

*

We are so rooted in space recognition
That size has blinded us to what dynamics mean—
We become so used to putting sizes in order
That we fail to comprehend significance--
Until we respond to essence
We will bump into, and miss
A world and its show—
The big is compact in the small
The small overwhelms the big—

Size is only important
When we let comparisons confuse us--

*

It is so easy to fall
Into comparisons—
We accept
What others approve
For our lives--
Based on their comparisons
We struggle for identity—

*

Comparisons are putting strange thoughts
Into our minds—
We live in moments so unique
Ours can be the only experiences—

*

To be out of tune
With absurdity
Is to be out of touch
With reality—

*

What are you seeking
When you strive for excellence?
Excellence is someone else's definition—
What does your voice say?
Does it have to do
With someone else's achievement?
No one is capable of excellence—
We achieve our individual limits--
How does that begin to satisfy
What your efforts would be?

*

Weight is immaterial
Distance is a distraction
Time is a contest
That only "now" subdues—

*

In civilization
Everything is weighed and measured—
Do you want to live like that?

Once we are shaped by science
We are not free--

*

Why are our minds

Producing contradictions?
What fantasies must we come up with?
Nature is a continuous unrolling--
Every result is contingent on what went before—
No disjunction, no reversal—
A strawberry does not give birth
To a pineapple
A salmon does not produce
A golden retriever—
All comes predictably
Out of what was preparation for it—
Contradiction is our jumping to conclusions
And failing to see connections--

Certainly the world is steeped
In variation—
But we investigate so carelessly
That it appears as unseen leaps
And landings—
We give value to every comparison
So much so
That they fight and curse one another
In an anonymous world--
They threaten values
Others have deemed important—
We accept the jagged moment
Instead of following the natural flow—

*

That cloud is present for all to see
Yet everyone has his own version
Of what it looks like—

*

To speak
The language of clouds
Is to speak
In god's tongue--

*

Where is god
When the sky is blue?
He walks
Upon the plushest carpets
The most intricate rugs—
His feet, his beautiful feet
Always seen
Disappearing—
Where is he now?

*

A dark sky
With clouds carrying the light—
Lo! Lightning flashes—

*

I am photographing so many clouds
They are becoming just clouds—
Blessed, blessed clouds—
I see one now—

*

A wispy cloud
Going fifteen miles an hour
Is leaving far behind
The westward speeding moon—

*

On the road all day
I never reached
That cloud—

*

I can't go on living like this—
Nothing to show for it but change—

*

The world shuffles
At its own insufferable pace—

*

The desert sands
Bury daylight in darkness
Grain by grain—

*

Men give names to hills—
Hills give character to men—

*

A journey of a thousand miles
Begins with a billion starting steps—

*

Where do mountain roads go?
They don't go nowhere—
They go round the mountain
And they don't come back—

*

I expand
As my world gets smaller—
I will be out of reach
If it gets any tighter—

*

A little breeze
A little blossom
A little flying bug—
A little oddity
A little kindness
A little unexpected delight—
We dare not get
Too big for ourselves—

*

ACCOMPLISHMENTS

We sip a sample of that
We partake of a token of that
We airily visit a site
We've waited a lifetime to see
We strive to accomplish a Herculean chore
We snatch for fleeting answers—
And seldom settle within for ourselves—

*

Every leaf is a victory—

*

How many ships before
"Ships that pass in the night"?
How many leaves slip away

Before we see leaves falling?
The world of plentiful numbers
Happens in solitary strokes--

*

On automatic pilot now
We don't remember
The decisive actions taken
Years before—

*

People who are
Seldom know who they are—

*

Desire is half of life—
Indifference is most of death—
Desire races toward surprise—
Indifference swoons at death's door—

*

Tired people
Are pre-occupied
With tired things—

*

Are you being drawn to the center
Or are you the center
People are drawn to?

*

The furious threaten less danger
Than the quiet straining under pressure—

*

We seldom acknowledge
The paradise we live in
But robbed of it
Our loss is sore—

*

We can't have a better friend
Than nature—

*

The journey to relevance
Is the path to now—
If we can live in the now
Fully accepting and appreciating it
We will be in discovery

And live to advantage—

*

We lose relevance
Soon after birth—
Somehow we hardly miss it
Until we begin to value it
As death approaches—

*

Living now
Is to be in command—
We have only now
A now that stretches
Into eternity--

*

Life must sustain life—
Art beauty to excess
Is lifeless—

*

When one is living now
Art and everything else

Is incidental—
What we need to be fully alive
Is now
To be aware of this moment
This one pure moment—
That is all
That is eternity—

*

Why would anyone approach nature
With metaphor
When it's variety is beyond all description!

*

Where we are
Is the beginning
Or the end—
Now is so elusive
It's impossible to capture—

*

"Extreme present"
Is a drag—
Stay with now--

*

How can it be atom size
When it is exploding?
Each moment so finite
That promise seems lost—
Now now now
The eternal present so huge
It never can be gotten beyond—

This glorious moment
Now now now—
The turtle winning the race
Never crossing the goal--
That moment, the dot
Disappearing into the finish line
To exist forever--

*

We follow
And pick up
Episodes of scattered eternity—
We expect it to lead us home--
Some of it so sweet
Some weighing us down
Some sparkling
For long trips or short
For walking, stumbling
Dancing and feasting—

Strange, we are so attached
To our returning—

*

We don't produce art
Because we're involved
In the business of living—
It's a struggle merely to keep up
With what we're doing--

*

The beginning of the year—
The minutes of the day don't move—
The pages of the daily calendar
Lurch into moving—

*

My daily calendar says
I should cherish each moment
Then it prints one page
For the two-day weekend—

*

Today is the nineteenth
Because tomorrow is the twentieth
And yesterday was the eighteenth—

That all time should revolve`
Around the nineteenth—
Nothing is more amazing
To be less inconsequential!

*

Routine—
Tables on Wednesday
Seats on Thursday
Floors on Friday
And then it happens!

*

Every day is the hundredth anniversary
The hundredth second
Of someone's momentous feat—
It is happening all the time—

*

A noisome fly
Humming, buzzing
At my window
Beats its wings
345 strokes a second--
Time is a paper tiger--

*

A dragonfly darts
At our speeding car—
Its shadow breaks in
And disappears again—

*

The present can be unappealing
Without the past—
The trick is to ignore the past
So the present can shine--

*

Don't worry—
Your needs of today
Won't be your needs of tomorrow—

*

Zen calendars
Never start, never stop—
Zen calendars
Don't tell time—

*

The clock on the wall
Says 7:15—
The clock right next to it

Says a quarter to five—
Both are correct—
Time is an illusion
Or at best
A reflection in a bathroom mirror
Of what we vainly attempt to control—

*

"It's eight o' clock," I said
Meaning our balcony visit was over—
"It's eight o'clock," R said
Meaning he was starting breakfast--
"It's eight o'clock—"
Meaning the day was proceeding—
Simple has the most meanings—

*

A wrist watch only mimics time
No matter how often
Its hands circle its face—
We partition our deeds with words
Every time we see those crazy hands—

*

Time hurried
Is time wasted, time lost—
"Cramming in" means

Loss somewhere else—
Time is a gaming device—
It behaves strictly
And leaves us flat out of luck—

*

Fantasy is the strongest fact
Of measured time—

*

Stop with all this goddamned time!
We're too much of time—
Kindness erases time—
All that is revered and good
Dissolves time in meaninglessness—
Love is timeless—
Oh holy seasons turning
Oh sublime sun rising
Even if we take no heed of it
Oh gorgeous bird song
Even if we don't recognize it
Oh astonishing leaf blowing
Along the sidewalk—
Whose time are we fitting into?
We needn't give it another thought!

*

We are hounded by time!
When did we let time
Get control of us!

*

We are pure science—
A mixture of measure and absurdity—

*

Restraining time
Makes a wild beast of it—
Pulling, yanking on the leash
It is adaptable at best
When we are strong--
The weaker we become
The more obstreperous it is—
Then we are pinned to the ground
And time is at our throats—

*

We seem unable to treat time
Seriously—
We dress it as the suppliant jester--
Given our lack of attention
It switches to masked villain—

*

The earth is timeless—
Man is time—

*

The earth is ageless—
We do our best
To keep up—

*

It is timeless
And now it's...
Now...now...never was—

*

Forget that butterfly in the Andes—
My nose itches
Because of the president
Of these United States--

*

The now is the only test
Of bliss, enlightenment, success—
Tomorrow is another test—

*

Help! I'm a prisoner of now—
The word seizes me—
And you?
What is more now than you
If you capture every moment of it—

*

"Now" has been encrusted
With so many ideas
We don't know
What its core conceals—

*

Now is the meaning—
If it isn't now
There is no meaning—

*

THE BUS STOPS HERE

*

The moment has passed—
It is always now—
It is all we have—

*

What you're doing now
Affects the world
For fifty billion years
And maybe more—
Only you will know--

*

The world is so slippery—
Between now and then
Between here and there
Between instant and eternity
Stability never finds a foothold—

*

Now
Makes all the difference—
What we do
Now
Determines the direction we go--
The world of infinite possibilities
From grains of sand on the floor
From floods of rain
Falling from the sky
Now—
We've little time to decide—

*

If we don't remember
That it ever happened
Did something exist?
The past gets smaller with time--

*

If all is change
If nothing stays the same
What is history?

*

In the archives of the earth
Are hidden
The most precious memories
So rare, so valuable, so meaningful
When they are glimpsed—
They disappear
As fast as they appear
They are forgotten
And not missed—
They are nothing—
Did you catch that moment?
It is yours to savor
Only this instant—

*

While memory can prize
Its value is gold—
Eventually it is dust to dust—

*

Why does the past always seem so drab
When we know color was everywhere?
Everything fades with distance—
Now now now—

*

Anything compared to gold is bizarre—

*

Now is a thin shell
Cresting all of yesterday—
Details fade—
If the past were as vivid as today
We'd continue to live it—
Unable to escape those details
We'd toil in a festering past—

*

We understand little
Of time and space—
We hardly qualify

As figments of our imagination--

*

The world hangs
By a gossamer:
By mistake
I am right
As often
As I am wrong
By certainty--

*

What do you see?
The world has changed
In half an hour!
Impossible!
The world has been the world
For millions of years
And changes
Before the "i" is dotted—

*

You need witness, collaboration
That the world has changed?
When did you stop breathing?

*

Time atoms burst
All around us—
We want to share their delight with everyone--
We have a grasp on some we want to share
And they have theirs to share—
Oh why do we think there's too little to share?
While we pass each other
In our somber magisterial robes—

*

I sit on the balcony
For brief, quiet minutes--
What a waste of time--
I don't sit long enough—

*

There he was
A man on a balcony
Scouring a chair
Scrubbing the universe—

*

CROSS PURPOSE STRIPES

Below a sunlit railing
An awning ripples
With stripes other than its own--

*

The balcony shadows
Have sprouted wings
And are preparing to fly—

*

The view from the balcony
Is perfect—
The view from the balcony down the way
Is perfect—
The view from every balcony is perfect—
Nothing is more obvious than perfection--

*

In this moment, horsefly
You are perfect—
No other moment is necessary—

*

The little ego of my mind
Tacks pictures on my wall
And then the wall is torn down

And then the ocean advances
330 feet deep
And whozeewhatzee fish
Are my favorite--
And still my mind goes on--
I trust I'm not crowding you—

*

The countdown
To what?
Begins—
The countdown
Never stops--
The countdown
Is illusion--

*

Get ready, get set, go—
Wind chimes sound the mark—
The world begins—

*

Delight in the obvious—
It is virgin territory--

*

As soon as we recognize
Ordinary life
It morphs into diamonds—

*

Recognition affirms perfection—

*

Perfection is defined by how closely
An object conforms to our needs—
A perfect cup of coffee
A perfect bonsai tree—
Usually the larger a project is
The less perfect it is
Too many cooks muddy the soup—
The less we know about it
The more likely we are to call it perfect
A god perhaps--
Taking all considerations into account
We might consider perfection a relative thing—

*

The exuberant leaves of youth
Nourish thirsting mind more
Than solemn ceremonial teas do—

*

I expect
Afternoons of perfect tranquility—
Sunshine and breezes
And perfumed lilies wafting—
I expect, and get them
Most of the time—
They're available for everyone too—

*

Children run
For the sheer joy of it—
Adults need a reason—

*

Sitting or walking
Racing or reclining
We're always on the way—

*

Swimming, driving, flying, sledding
Running, skiing, diving, skating—
Walking can't be beat—

*

Walking is timeless—
We do not walk

Past a mountain in a day—
The important
(And what's not important?)
Means involvement—
But don't give time meaning—
All things in good time
Timeless—

*

Walking home in the snow—
The way is pristine ahead of me--
I will not turn my head
To see my tracks behind me—

*

"Hello, hello" said the soles of his shoes
As he receded down the street
Until I could no longer hear them—

*

Walking with an artist
Is like walking
With an inquisitive dog—
Enough time isn't available
To learn all that's there—

*

I'm becoming more doglike
In my everyday walks—
When I am totally dog
I will have succeeded--

*

To many dogs
A leash is not a leash—

*

Dandelions, daffodils, and tulips
Oh my!
On my way to the grocery store—

*

If our walk doesn't lead
To revelation
We haven't been paying attention—

*

Disparity jolts us
When we read about living
But do not live—
Acting is fulfillment--

*

If you don't think
Life is an adventure
Writing headlines for a living
Is a waste of time—

If you don't think
Life is an adventure
You'll never make it
As a newspaper reporter—

If anyone cares
Let it be the least said
In your newspaper notice
That you were in fact born—

*

Without action
There is no time—
Without action
There is no now
There is no meaning--

*

Everyone travels in his own time capsule—
It hardly credits a tall tree
That it has managed to live so long—

Tomorrow gives another meaning
To the journey—

*

Every generation faces
The most demanding times—
Futures carry the dead weight from the past
That we refuse to let go—
Habit and law protect the established—
We see sureness in the present
Beyond the tantalizing future—
We do not trust our genius—

*

Pleasure
From continuing to continuing—
Not short of the mark
Not overshooting the mark--

*

In time
Meandering roads become
Direct paths—

In time

Meandering roads become
One path--

*

The world is so hypnotic
Why doesn't it seduce us utterly
And enslave or destroy us?
We are obliged to survive
So we can participate completely—
We might say, "Do your damnedest, world!
We will take all you have
And give it back to you—"
*

We say the subject is the inspiration—
But it is our openness to receiving--
Response is to invite surprise—

*

Watts did not discover steam—
He did not search for it—
It became ever present
And he received it—

*

"That which is, is—
Do not search—

Stop and see—"   Osho

*

Nature characteristically
Tells us all about itself—
We are confused by its wealth
Being so in our face—
Its truth is there
Unadorned and unhidden—
We do not see it—
It is too obvious to be seen—
It is all mystery--

*

Crossing over—
In rushing youth
Time always is so far ahead—
In time it crowds around
And loses dimension—

*

THE WHITE RAINBOW

Like the moon that is hidden from view
But there
Like the moon that is distant
But there

Like the moon that is there
But unobserved
We are present
And gone
We and matter--
Our urgency about the same—

*

As a still pond will break
From something within
So does even emptiness erupt
With being from within—
If everything comes out of nothing
If life comes out of inanimate
What more is there to think about?
Questions are futile—
Answers only add to the mystery—
Questions and answers
Are the tension on the pool--
Faith comes out of questions unaskable—

*

The sparkle was created
By motion alone
Nothing else—

*

Something sticks
Something gathers
Something is real
Something melds—
The subtle ill-arrangement
The indiscriminant dots and dashes
The piles and spreads
The lines, the off-balance
The clumps and awkward stretches
Whatever it means
Whatever it suggests
It is you—
You will never see this again
Whether you wish to or not—
It is beautiful
And you know it—
Whatever materials
Whatever value
Whatever permanence
Whatever dimension
It is yours, never to see again—

*

Without wonder
Existence is without life—

*

Wonder has a source beyond us—
We shouldn't try to define it
We shouldn't try to own it—

*

Wonder is not diminished
By seeing a red atomic ball
Sink below a flat horizon line
Of a round circling planet—
No science vocabulary is enough--
Wonder is enhanced by knowledge--

*

To doubt life is a miracle
Is to drag for every breath—

*

What is the most amazing event
You can think of?
Right now finding 29 cents
In the debris of a house being razed—
Second most amazing
Third most amazing—
It makes no difference—
Amazing is not ranked or categorized
Nor listed in length of influence—

When you say "amazing," that's it—
Amazing is—

*

The moles, slugs, ants
Ignore or dig around
Pennies, nickels, and dimes
At the abandoned house--
They never wonder how they got there—

*

Birds track across
The trash strewn yard--
Pennies are stepping stones—

*

Our minds are our last instruments
For making our world safer—
Our minds are the first cause
Perpetuating our danger—

*

The most advantaged
As is so often correctly stated
Are the most successfully duped—

Failures feel their dissatisfaction to be final—
Both, for whatever reasons
Attribute damages as their due—

*

Delivering the morning paper
The man has all the news he needs—
The waning moon—

*

You feel no urgency?
You're too far away—
Distance discourages connection
And instills complacency--

*

Our conscious contact with something
Needn't change it—
But whatever it was
Now it is something else—

*

We know we should eat our daily bread
As if it were our last

As if it were the best of a great feast—
We know, but we take so little time—

*

If you're looking
For a reliable character reference
Refrigerators best document
The quality of our lives—

*

Domestic responsibilities
Make for alert minds—

*

Successful parties
Demand
Designated dishwashers—

*

As shredded as it may be
A dishwashing sponge
Still does the job--

*

"Another drink?"
"No more for I—"

*

A kitchen is not a kitchen
When perfectly clean—
Dirty cups
Denoting hospitality
Are the criterion—

*

A cup of tea:
Civilization
In four words—
In two words:
Tea ceremony—

*

A cup of tea can astonish the world
A flower arrangement arriving late
Can disrupt the world--
Oh the inconsequential monuments
Bestriding this world—

*

A tea cup's stain

Just about describes
Our lives—

*

The tea cup's stain
Says as much
As all the world's words—

*

We must never
Throw something away
If we don't know what it is--
When it's gone
It will prove to be an irreplaceable part
Of a vital gewgaw—
We know of course
That the problem is:
We've been made into
Incorrigible neatniks—

*

It doesn't matter
What quality a car is
When it's dirty--

*

No more beauty resides
In the collected museum treasures
Than in the waste filled gutters
Of our aggrieved cities—
Beauty is universal—
We need the perspective
Not to ignore it—

*

Life is so blessed—
Anything blessed has nothing to do
With time—
I sit, reading poetry—
That is miracle—
Out the window on the west
The day is gloomy gray—
But I swear
When I got up to look up a word
Was it seconds, minutes
The sun was shining in my north window—
Two windows, two lives—
How to quantify them—
All deliberate haste
Is beside the point—
The tip of the mountain
Rests on all the earth below—

*

Love with a name starts
With a love of nature—
Everything so included--

*

The moon soothes our stress
The sky relieves our doubts
The sun boosts our lives
The night eases our pain—
And time resolves our fear—
Prescriptions seldom do as well—

*

If we can't enjoy the moon
We're not living—

*

Across a sky
The moon where it is
Particularly—

*

The moon, at any time
Any phase, any place—

The moment of surprise—

*

I didn't think to look
For the waning moon—
It's like the goodbyes
We neglect to say
That prove to be the last—

*

Would you want to be alive
At any time but right now?

*

The moon knows
The seasons know
The mountains know
The trees know—
We see and hear
And don't pay attention—
They have their ordained paths
And have confounded us for centuries—
We present them as newest triumphs
As if we hadn't stolen them—

*

The Big Bang
Meaning no disrespect
Popped from a kernel of haiku—

*

What
Before a little word
Started
The Big Bang?

*

Startled by a frog
Plopping into a pond
The poet drops his brush—
Sparkling drops of water
Flood every fleeting moment—

*

How satisfying
Drawing water
Chopping wood—
More than miraculous this—
Satisfying—

*

Few of us are expedient
When faced with a Gordian Knot—
We fee, fiddle, fidget
Rather than cut
To the heart of the matter—

*

Who's to say we wasted yesterday
If we get on with today?

*

JUST THAT

Mixing and reforming forever
Life is a caldera of glass shards--
Just that--

*

Nature is of no plan
And yet
What better can we do
Than follow nature's course?

*

Tick tock tick tock—
The shadow of the palm tree

Season by season, year by year
Swings back and forth, back and forth
Across the street—
Tick tock tick tock--

*

The palm fronds say
"Yes, no, maybe
Maybe, no, yes
Maybe, maybe, maybe—"
That's what the tropics do—

*

I walk across
The early tree tops
To catch the sun—
I step upon the moon
For greater speed—
Winter is behind me--

*

Travel a narrow trail long enough
And it becomes wider and wider
Even as we pass burned out patches—
War-torn landscapes, pestilence
And trafficking in humans—

Happiness must be part of us
Or we can be no help to others--
Happiness is salvaged
Even on the rockiest trail—

*

It is not gravity--
We could soar forever
If it weren't for life below—

*

We are whip-lashed
By the leaves and stems
Of immediacy—
Stable roots and trunks
Have no time
For such indulgence—

*

The train whistle in the distance
Is part of nature—
The whirl of the electric fan
Is part of nature—
The faucet dripping
The chair foam poofing

When someone sits
Is part of nature—
Otherwise is separation--

*

We are eating away at eternity
With a tea spoon--
Our appetites are unsatisfied--
Tomorrow's feast will be as wanting—

We are eating away at eternity
With a tea spoon—
We are prepared to think
This is how nature intended us to feed—

*

The world goes on
As always—
Our minds give us
So much importance—

The mind is odd man out
Confusing civilization
With elemental activity—

*

From randomness
Purpose is perceived—
Randomness is a proof of order—
Randomness no less than order—

*

Watch
How that crow weaves
Back and forth
Over that long vacant distance—
He is aiming for that goal over there
Or that spot far separate
Heaven knows where
Over there—

*

The farther off the bird's destination
The more important it seems—
Funny how our minds work—

*

A bird flying without purpose
Our purpose?
Its purpose?
Enlarges our lives—

*

Chaos is as ordered
As order is—
Our own disorder
Seldom is seen that way—

*

Birds flying in utter randomness
That we can see
Suddenly assume order
That we can see—
There has to be sense to it—
But no more than what was
Before or after—

*

Yes, the flight of birds affect
The drift of clouds—
Yes, our thoughts affect
The outcome of history—
Yes, they can be in conflict
With our rambling thoughts—

*

A bird
Flying alone

Is never flying
Alone—

*

One bird
Flying alone
Is all the truth
We need to know—

*

Space for hovering birds
Is what poetry is for adaptable men—

*

Hi-tech achievement
Can't begin to equal
A gull's drift in aimless flight—

*

Birds could sense
Their fingers were disappearing—
Did they say, "Go for it?"
In time did they know
It was too late to stop
And make the best of it?
Would they fly with a heavy heart

Intuiting they had lost so much
But were still be able to fly
With the joy of a lark—

*

Flying in a squadron
Is not as easy as it looks—
It took millions of years
To develop so casual a flow—
The weight of feathers, muscles, and bone
And all that's inside—
Our lives need quicker solutions—
We haven't got as much time--

*

Airplanes are born
Out of the clouds—
You doubt it?
Put 4 and 5, and 100 to a 1,000,000
And 1,000,000,000's to 1,000,000,000's
And you've got clouds
Introducing airplanes
That now are in the 1,000's—
Proof, QED, quod erat demonstrandum—

*

"That airplane high in the sky

Has wings—"
"That's a bird—"
"That's an airplane—"

*

If birds were possessive
How much they would own—
If we could escape possessing
How rich we'd be in sharing—

*

Wobbling through the air
That bird is drunk!
Drunk on pure essence--

*

Birds are the fortune tellers
Of the sky—
Full of mystery
Full of potential—
Tea leaves--
Watch them swoop
Those clusters of conspiracy
Those pivoting priorities
A sudden reversal
A uniform progression
Swirling furies

Gracious sprites--
A solo gathering of condition--
What's your story?
What's your fate?
You cannot escape them—
The fortune telling birds
Are subjects too--

*

We choose our sages
With more care than we suspect—
We learn by charisma—
The flight of birds—

*

Shrinking smaller and smaller
In this world—
We're part of a flock
Changing color and direction
In the sky—

*

If all a bird had to do
Was fly
If all a flower had to do
Was bloom
If all rain had to do

Was fall
If all a man had to do—
Is he distracted
With so much mental posturing?

*

Against the thunder's rumble
A bird's chirp—

*

Birdie
You cannot help reminding us
There is nothing to fear
That everything will turn out fine—
We suspect that's not true—
But we're not the most intelligent
creatures—

*

We are two birds
Meeting on a branch--
We fly away—
We are two people—

*

Over one house
Through a backyard
Two birds flying
Ten feet apart
As if wedded
As much in love--

*

The early bird doesn't get the worm—
He waits outside in the cold
Until the store opens—

*

None of us counts all your feathers
Or says your toenails need clipping
But our interest, sparrow
Matches god's—

*

Birds are an antidote
Nature is a tonic—

*

A feather's impact on the ground
Causes the earth to quake—

Where does ennui come from?

*

Feed a worm and feed the world—

*

The first important date
In human history is
The discovery of flowers—
And how many eras had to pass
Before we deigned
To put the fragile things in vases?

*

An orchid, a weed
A daisy, a rose
Bloom for us—

*

A blossom gives the world
Courage, peace, and love—
Yet so few of us are alert
To this message—

*

Blossoms
Do not
Waste
Time—

*

A blossom knows
When to die—
Wisdom
Is part of its beauty—

*

Somewhere
A flower is blooming for us—
Somewhere
Flowers are blooming
In such profusion
We must wonder
How we can be so deserving—

*

Every blossom we discover
Is a blessing—
Could we but imagine
How many we don't find--

*

Some plants' sole purpose
Seems to be to produce blossoms—
Perhaps that's the artist's too—

*

Flora everywhere—
We don't need
Just blossoms--

*

Slender stems carry moisture
To blossoms—
Clear necessity
Travels to the artist's brain—

*

We are as house plants
Doing our everyday thing
But a knob is growing
Tighter and more persistent--
It make us uncomfortable—
It pops through
A leaf, an idea—

*

Creativity

Displaces banal refinement—
We do not mock a source—
We know the lotus rises from the muck—
Creativity springs from contrast—
Eventually an ethereal god
Springs from a sullied source--

*

The tiniest blossom
Cannot be disparaged—
Infinity starts
In the heart of a blossom—

*

A geranium's happiness
Caps the world—

*

Blossoms exude perfume
All their existence—
Oh sweet luxury
Given to the world—
How can anything so precious
Be so freely given?
The humility of the gift
That astounds us all
With its free flowing glory—

We give to the world
Expecting it to be
Less than we are—
But there we are
Gifts so small
But greater than we can be—

*

Wild flowers
Show us the way
The road must go—

*

A suitcase in the trash—
The journey
Is almost over—

*

Weeds are the salvation
Of every neglected and forgotten place--

*

What aesthete Master
Positioned this garbage dump
Beneath this rusting trestle

Straddling this untended garden site?

*

The world is filled with beauty--
Men cannot defile it—

*

Plants are bestowals of virtue—
When we try to possess them
They become the source of mischief--

*

In a robust field
Destruction can be well concealed—
When conflict intrudes
Anything appears to expire—

*

What does it matter
If we have found ways
To prevent war
If we can't find peace
With nature?

*

My garden grows
Until it is wild with weeds—
I bring it back
To conformity with civilization—
Coming and going
Going and coming
My gift to the world—
Not all gifts are recognized—
Mine is no less a gift
For being unknown—

*

Florida used to be
Savannahs, hamlets, razor grass
Alligators—
I assume that's not true
But I am not knowledgeable enough
To see the difference—

Bring it back, bring it back—
I will weave of growing grasses
I will walk wherever I must go—
Oh bring it back, bring it back—
Too late, too late—

*

The world attempts to give us
So much bounty

(That none can take away)
And we do our blind best
To refuse it—

*

Vines will grow
Along slinky fences
And lounge on sagging roofs—
Some will grow
Up slender poles
And attempt arching bridges—
And some will reach
The tops of dying trees—
Opportunity draws us all—
Nature mostly, and opportunity—
Opportunity chooses our paths
And nature provides our means—

*

Do I differentiate between
Myself and a bougainvillea blossom?
You betcha—
Do I argue there's difference
Between a bougainvillea blossom and me?
We betcha—

*

Bougainvillea was losing
The blossom competition—
Its tiny blossoms
Were less and less an insect's goal—
What could it do!
A larger blossom would make it more desirable—
Instead, it developed colorful leaves
Like luscious petals
To surround the modest blooms
And deceive—
We masters of foolery
How casually we fool living things—

*

That bougainvillea reaching
From down there
To up here
Is as demanding of a story
As Macbeth, Agatha Christie, or Sam Spade—

*

The bougainvillea blossoms are reaching
Beyond their limits—

Any farther and they will be floating—
They are...floating--

*

My lost glasses
Are in the garden--
They're staring at me
All the time—

*

The night isn't long enough
For the palm trees to dance—
The day isn't so poor in exuberance
That they can't celebrate—
They're our formal models
For proclaiming
Our closeness to creation—

*

When winter lurks
I do not complain
About palm trees' skimpy shadows—

*

How cautious spring is—
A bit of green here and...
There—
A migrating bird hiding
Behind a slender waving branch
Where all but the bird can be seen—
A blossom, startling in its placement
In shadow covering gloom—
We think spring is so bold—
But look, did you see it?
It was here, it is gone—
You only thought you saw it--
And now it is everywhere—

*

Do not think badly of me
Water, trees, clouds—
Every moment I can
I try to do
What is gentle and non-destructive—
I try to leave the world
Unchanged—

*

In this minimal room
A bonsai and I
Compete to love—
Love does not compete—

This bare room invites love—

*

Imagine the courage
To engage with a bonsai
That has a million years
Head start—

*

Flowers cannot, will not
Give up
Their simplicity, their transience—
Therein is their beauty—

*

Flowers cannot be dissected with words--
Harsh words toward the helpless
Are barbarous—

*

If I were the tiniest blossom
In the sun or out
I could not be happier—
Presence is happiness is love—

*

A spray of grass takes
As much initiative
To be a spray of grass
As it takes a sprig of child
To be a person—

*

The genius flower
Indulges
The inept gardener--

*

Anyone who can choose a blossom
From his garden
Is in control of his life—

*

Your garden
Is only cracks
In the sidewalk?
How rich you are!

*

Our servitude to civilization is
Too obvious to see or defend—
The Jewish servitude in Egypt

Was no worse
Than what we all suffer today
In cultured society—

*

If you're not taking
At least twice as long
To finish your gardening chores
You're not taking advantage
Of your garden's gifts—

*

If you haven't received
A spring garden catalog
Go to a hardware store and read
A dozen vegetable seed packets—
Bon Appetite--

*

At the ocean's edge
The first wave ever
Breaks upon the shore—

*

In a fountain's waterfall
The splashing, gurgling sounds

Gambol to be fully understood—
Listen--
The meaning will come to you--

*

Ever spilling the fountain's pool
The putti's tears
Are jewels of joy--

*

SHAPING ONE'S SELF TO CIRCUMSTANCES

Hands cupping water--
Water, the civilizing influence--
Harmonizing water--
Church of the living water--
Strong like water--
Flow like water--

*

Catch it!
The most important moment
Of all time—
A drop of water
Falling—

*

THE SEQUIN SEA

*

WATER RESTORES THE THIRSTING SOUL

*

Love being a raindrop
On a leaf—
We are fantastical creatures—
We are flying loose
Thinking we are the center
Of a mindless universe—

*

The ocean is fed
By many rivers—
This is not to say
They are its only sustenance—
But no source can be ignored—

*

FLOW LIKE WATER

We are guided
To expend our energy
Just as a stream is ushered

Downward, around rocks, around mountains
The water principle
Its momentum stopped
By a landslide or avalanche
Until it overcomes and flows its natural way—
Perhaps majestically as it waters vast fields
And prosperous wide lands—
Perhaps it is renewed
In falls and white water courses
Maybe it finds
A fortuitous way to flow—
Sometimes, mysteriously it disappears
Into sucking earth--
Sometimes it can go no farther--
It reaches a dead sea
And fulfills a mythic destiny--
Maybe it reaches that luminous place
In the ocean--
Guided, driven, forced
The river always claims its law and right—

*

The world goes its own way—
As I look toward the waterway
A tall-masted boat approaches the bridge—

I look at my watch—
On schedule the bridge is going up—
The world is perfectly synchronized
And it isn't even for me!

*

Let it be noted
That I was one of the first hundred thousand
Who crossed the bridge
When it opened for traffic—

*

On a busy bridge
The sidewalk
Never is wide enough—

*

The fixed flag is going faster
Than its boat traveling nowhere—

*

A tugboat can be
The rewarding object
In our sight—

Providence places
One bright star
In the all black sky—

*

A wader steps into a pool—
Whatever the pool's size
The water is stirred—

*

I LAUGH, THEREFORE I AM

*

GOOD NATURED MEN

*

Taking life seriously, or:
Losing one's way
When life is beyond absurdity—

*

Whatever our confusion or heartache
We travel to the end
As dumb as when we began—

Our brightest moments pass hilarity
And reach absurdity—

*

Don't we realize
Everything said
Makes sense—
Why would we reject
Absurdity!

*

One person's mind
Crazy!
Two people's minds
Absurdity!

*

If we never laughed
At what was to be taken seriously
We might never laugh—
Laughter is safe only among peers—
Out of class and we're in danger—
Till Eulenspiegel and the king's fool
May be the only ones to get away with it—
We jest, we must laugh—
Laughter is the only way we can be sure

Something can be made right—
Be brave—
Democracy is laughter—
Laughter is freedom—
Laughter is the flame lapping
Around an iceberg's scowl—

*

If a clown can steal your composure
You're a greater fool than he—
Embrace him—
Show him he has met his brother—

*

We don't cotton being the fool—
We play the role without conviction
But with great skill--
When we don't care
What people think of us
They naturally think of us
As fools
And all's right with the world—

*

Being called a fool
Is not an insult—

Good folk know
That's our nature—

*

We are taken for fools!
How perceptive people are—
And yet, so few comfortably wear
The title themselves--

*

THE FLY WALKING DOWN THE STAIRS

Distraction is responsible
For more humor and danger
Than we dare admit—

*

Unless we can look
At the world's foibles
With mild amusement
We're hardly engaged in life—
Laughter confirms experience—

*

While bubbles slosh

About in our brains
Serious ballast is protected—

*

How can we spring to life
If we are without the resilience
Of humor?

*

FOOL'S CAP

Wisdom comes
Unnoticed, unannounced—
However diligently one searches
Effort and study are wasted—

Like random results in a field
Some heads ripen to wisdom
Unexpected, undeserved—
Time itself is an interloper—

No one knows a wise youth
And so often old wisdom lies fallow—

If one is wise
He can think himself blessed

As all the while

Wisdom tells him he wears a fool's cap—

*

NOMINA STULTORUM SUNT UBIQUE LOCORUM

*

When we are consistently funny
People begin to recognize
That we are philosophers
Who have chosen to live
On the sunny side of the street—

*

A humanist doesn't have
Any other standards
For gauging the human comedy
Than his own--

*

Absolutely nothing
Is quicker to cause laughter
Than certainty defended—

*

Laughing with each other
Is more satisfying
Than crying together--

*

Light heartedness
Often has us reading
Comic strips
We wouldn't read before—

*

Humor is like a snake
Slithering through tall grass—
Eventually it bites us
On the ass—

*

Cheap humor
Has a steep price--

*

Did you hear about the man
Who lost his speech
And then when it was restored
Years later
Had nothing to say?

He explained
Self-education
Had much improved him--
People were riled—

*

"I'm thinking of writing my next book
In Sanskrit--"
"Yes, you could write it in sand
And have a book signing at the beach--"

*

"Naked Lunch—"
He should have tried "Naked Brunch—"
"Naked Buffet" might have done it—
"Naked Snack at Midnight"
Is more like it—

*

We keep looking for wisdom—
So often in staid and proper places—
It keeps showing up in the dust storms
And ironic comic strips—
Humor finds wisdom
In the unlikeliest places—

*

An artist must breathe
Humor
Or he is not human—

*

By habit I read the editorials
Just before I enjoy the comics—
Have followed this sequence for years—
No one's given me a more satisfying plan—
The two are not interchangeable
No matter what you say--

*

We answer guardedly
We answer with a joke
To another's openness—
How often do people speak openly?
In our defense, it is often fear that starts
As showing off, from early school days—
Now we're all full-blown part-time comics
But cheerful all the while—
That has to count for something—

*****

ART

Art comes out
Of the blue
And returns
Into the black—

*

Art is shorthand
For what often enough
We can't make sense of--

*

Art—
We don't know
What we are missing—

*

Art conjures space—
We adjust accordingly—

*

Art attempts
With harlequin verve
To create fleeting full moons--

*

ART IS THE MOST IMMEDIATE EXPERIENCE

*

Art is reaching out—
How far is unpredictable--

*

Art does not have to reach—

*

Art is not justification—
If it doesn't flow naturally
It isn't art—

*

Art is breath unopposed—
Art is breath suspended--

*

Art is the lifeline thrown
To the drowning
When nothing else is available
To save him—

*

Art is the band-aide
Applied to the wounds
We inflict upon people
We love—

*

Art is the web
Upon which we communicate
Our hunger for another—

*

Like god touching Adam's finger
Art animates--
After that
Adam labors on his own--

*

Art isn't accuracy of line
Appropriately applied paint
Precision of form and composition—
It is the artist's temperament
Free of borders--

*

Art does not have to be a "perfect"
To be striven for—

It will be unrivaled
If it's of the artist's being
And following his own quest--
How will we be able to judge?
It will be as excellent
As anything need be—

*

Don't make effort
To be perfect
Beyond your own ability--
You will have it when you're you—

*

Art is relative
Trauma is relative
Character is relative
Craft is relative—
An artist is all of the above—

*

Art mimics the living
But survives as a mirror of the mind—
Art committing beauty to "timelessness"
Fails—

*

Art that demands
Isn't necessarily better—
Art that proposes
Might have the edge—

*

Art is adult toys--
It helps us learn and advance
Without imperiling our existence—

*

Art is emotion and intellect
Vicariously experienced--

*

Art is sparked by passion
Guided by intellect—

*

Art reaches a place
Where emotion and reason
Release difference—

*

In art we create the illusion
Of power and triumph--
Art convinces us of truth
Where the world seems false—
Where the world is oppressive
Art consoles us with healing—

*

Art is pernicious fiction
Lulling us into believing
Invention is better than real life—

*

Art is the con--

*

Art succeeds as art
When objections are inconsequential—

*

Art is search and preserve—
Craft is utility and expenditure—

*

Art is the indivisible part
Beyond craft—
The final result must be
A patient and well-plotted pleasure—
Art refined to minimum expression
Is the best art—

Some art is so clear in conception
An audience can only wonder
How it has escaped notice before
It is so simple, so obvious
That it can be apprehended immediately
And appreciated—
This should be true for geometry, physics, biology
For all arts as well—
If the art is clear, nothing stands between it
And satisfaction—

*

Every story starts
At the beginning of the world—

*

Sometimes
Art has no place for us

But at the very beginning—
It has nothing to do with originality--

*

Art is not eternal—
While perhaps ageless, it is not living—
Life always takes precedence--

*

Art crushes time and space—
But if it isn't more direct than life
Why would we call it art
And bother with it at all?

*

The toughness of art
Allays any softness of shell—

*

Art expresses a benevolence
That exists nowhere else
In printed cosmology--

*

Art's not worth much
If it can't thrive in cracks
And arid wastes—
Art survives
Conflict and neglect—
What's it worth
Without proving endurance
Without showing it must survive?

*

Art becomes increasingly esoteric—
Nature steps in and renews the old ways—

*

Art makes
Pressing nature
Palatable—

*

Art is life
Yet somehow
Completely foreign
To it--

*

Art captures a semblance of nature
Or it doesn't succeed—

*

Art pops up
After nature has had its say—

*

Art is not nature—
Nature is not art—
The intrusive artist
Makes the difference--

*

Art might be called the Great Soother—
Most art, if it can be called art
Is hardly the outcast disruptor
The iconoclast
The art with little popular acceptance—

Original art resists soothing time--
Familiarity is art's prime enemy—
Familiarity sucks the blood from art—

*

Some revere art
As a god—
For many art is
Santa Claus—

*

Skill and a questing mind
Are the vehicle to art renown—
It is character, unique and original
That holds the contraption together—

*

Art is a man's preening
To entice the only thing he needs
Someone's favor—

*

Art is prolongation
Of orgasm—

*

Art is an artist jumping
In sheer exuberance--
The artist leaps free
Of the world—

Landing is not his concern—

*

Art at its best
Is an attempt to show
Appreciation
For all the world has given us—

*****

THE ARTIST

THOSE SHINING LIGHTS

Somewhere a light will shine—
We will not know where
We will not expect it—
It will come
With no apparent necessity—
We may not see it—
We may think we're ready for it
We won't know if we're ready for it—
It may disappear
Unaccounted for—
No matter—
We know somewhere a light will shine—
Though we are looking for it
It is not our light—

Why are all those lights shining?
We do not speculate—
We do not doubt
Though we're struggling constantly
For that light to shine—
Somewhere at any time or place
It will shine
And have nothing to do with us—
A light will shine—
Why now?

Why here?
A light will shine—
It will be for us—
The light that always is shining—

*

All things are in us
And touch us not—
So much is known by us
And is veiled from us—
Light always is pressing in
Behind the dark—
In the blackest night
Light peeps in—
But it has flashed!
It is enough for us—
We have made a mark
Where none of us
Had made a mark before—

*

An artist is right on
Avoiding originality—
Most of the time
Originality is conforming
To the latest on the market—

An artist's work follows
From within him and is original—

*

We must be wary
Of the advice to look for truth—
We tend to assume the source comes
From outside us—
It doesn't—
Outside truth is large and confusing—
Ours is contained nowhere
But compact and deep
Inside our individual selves—

*

Young artists
At the only time in their lives
Have a naiveté to be
Their prickly selves—

*

NAÏVE IMAGINATION

The new, the unknown
The innocent
Without guile

Without purpose
Except to be
Without stability
Without guilt and concern
The new—

*

Nothing, nothing, nothing
Makes us predictably creative—
Each mind is so intrinsically intricate
That no one else can be
The exemplar we are—

*

The fuel combusting
In the artist
Burns the dying formulas--

*

The artist sees relevance
Beyond the aimless milling
Others are confused by—
An artist's opportune vision
Respects ordinary events
And presents them as sublime—

*

Creativity goes beyond intelligence
If passion doesn't derail it--
Follow it—
Catch it if you can—
Don't be afraid—

*

Passion is a flaring match—
Art bursts open and blinds us
In timelessness—

*

Passion crunches us
Against the accepted—
Maybe not correctly
But this is the way art goes—

*

PASSION OR DESIGN

Which do you prefer
Emotion on the sleeve
Or the maverick
Bubbling from inside?

*

The quiet person in the room
Is the artist—

*

An artist's
Active mind
Has all the time
In the world
For nothing—

*

It's hard to respect the new art
When it's the young making it—
What respect do kids get!

*

Every age begins its own origin—
It is the same old stuff
Poured into new bottles
Rearranged
On the same old shelf
Renovated—

*

Reform is a fact of life—

It will happen
At its own time and place
And severity—
It will happen
Defying all rank and rationality—

*

We accept the tart taste of the new
Only after it's been diluted
With the familiar tang of the old—

*

Copying other art:
It's too slow
It's too boring
And so second rate—
Certainly it never pays enough—
Better to try original—
Better to know thyself—

*

Crisis in painting!
Until the zealous personality comes along--

*

Traditionalists consider the past
Superior to the present
That's where they came from—
The aging young lions try to prove
The conservatives wrong
Even after they've forgotten
They're the accepted—

*

The world is filled with
Competents—
We choose a competent sandwich
At a franchise—
We select a competent shirt
At the department store—
We buy a competent chair
From the local furniture store—
Competent is the average attainment—
Anything better is unobtainable
For the average of us who can't keep up--
Thank god for us—
But the world changes
Through the awkward trials of artists—

*

The competents
Do it over and over—

Geniuses do it
Once--

*

People have been so deprived of artistic sense
That if they were given five cents of talent
They'd be considered geniuses—

*

Any unknown artist
Is fair game
For spurious speculation—

*

A re-evaluation of art is due—
An artist's name is not a rating—
Art's anonymous worth
Is unlikely to capture it--

*

To be an artist
Is to demand introspection—

An artist
Who warrants no introspection
Is not worth the time—

*

It's a shame artists have to be drawn
To world Meccas—
Their achievements
Were formed in conventional homes
In unusual ways—
However jumbled their art
It was born in pre-school settings
And was nourished there
No less worthy, no less fulfilling
Than in the art filled city ateliers
Where the crowd recognition is won—
Art perishes every day—
It is meant to perish
As more and more people are patrons
And all art is scattered and shared—
Local savants cannot save it all
And museums salvage only a part—
Shy art perishing everywhere
All the time
Is the world at its most normal—

*

So many of those fires

That smolder for years
Suffocated, dampened, deprived
Yet linger, hold on, survive
And burst into flame
Long after the fire has raged—
Their light is lost among the light—

*

My references belong
Fifty years in the past
But I cannot help
Being of my time—
The present is the air I breathe--

*

If an artist can't trust
His own style and taste
Is he an artist?

*

The artist's persistent threat
Is to let doubt dilute his efforts—

*

The more fractured the artist
The more disjointed his art—

Distressed art stimulates charity—

*

Creativity sticks close to commonplace
Except where the artist's life skews them—
It comes somewhere in life—
To the artists it comes early and strong—
It means value outside of life—
It means life out of balance—
It means looking for life within—

*

As long as we doubt
Our vision is not our own
That we're not seeing clearly
We never will be able to deal with others
Honestly in a full hearted way—
Whether artist, artisan, or average guy
Our independence of heart
Determines our fitness with the world—

*

An artist
If he knows something
About himself
Even when he doesn't fit
Comfortably in his element

Is an artist—

*

*

Some people never achieve
What they think is their rightful goal—
It simply is not within them—
Sometimes they never recognize
What's best in them—

*

What we were
Is not what we are—
What we will be
Is like nothing we were—
Direction and goal are as improbable
As the dice's roll—
Whose dice?

*

We are where we are--
We make the best of it—

*

We know how abstract "perfect" is—

We needn't give it any thought—
See how perfect we are—

*

Most of us argue
From values buried so deep
It isn't possible to say
We arrived at them
Without influence—
We lack the ability
To know where to question—
We find it difficult
To redirect our minds—

*

Circumstances have mated us
Perfectly to who we are—
We ask ourselves to change
And we are asked by others to change
But the world is too much within us—

*

Show me a lady who puts on
Powder, cologne, and lipstick
And I'll show you a female novelist—

*

Yes, the "anonymous artist" is a woman--
But also anyone of a quiet, reticent soul
Who has never pushed and spoken
Above a whisper—

*

If a woman has been instilled
With conventional womanly virtues
Is it possible for her to be the artist
A man is considered to be?

*

In this age of sexual parity
I hardly dare say
That artists require balls—
But a wee small voice inside says
"It's true—"
Balls disrupt--

*

Life's impacts can throw us out of whack—
Women often are art's victims--

*

Females are persuaded
By the idea of "Woman"

To be inflexible and strong
Or to be shrinking and pink—
In the process they lose
Their identity as the individual
They want to be—

*

Is it "the more serious the art
The more singular the quest?"
For women another desire
Seems to derail them—
As long as she must have children
She is compromised as an artist—

*

Children are the norm—
Art is the abnorm—

*

Men are just a comfort to women—
Men are an escape
From the chores of motherhood—

*

Men as play toys—
No wonder they fight so hard

To survive--

*

Men make women
Jump through hoops—
They push them to sing octaves above
Their comfort range
They make them raise pointed toes
Above their heads—
They depict their breasts sticking out
Of their shoulders
And their eyes popping
From behind their ears—
Men put them powerless
In the high places—

*

While countless paths exist
For an outsider to be an innovator
Homosexuality has to be a reliable one
Those insults and affronts to "normal
reality"—
Now society more easily accepts
That the outsiders and innovators
Seldom are synonymous with the normal—
Being gay doesn't have to be the reason
A person is an innovator
But it is as unsettling and erratic a platform

As any that creation bolts from—

*

Two young men walk together—
How long will it take
For them to know they love each other?

*

The sensitive female
The disorderly male
The homosexual artist--

*

We don't have to accept
What the media say—
We don't have to accept
What the well-meaning say—
What we have to say
Hardly is important
But it is the first to consider—

*

ENTRY LEVEL ECCENTRICS

*

My life is normal—
Our lives are normal—
They are present and here—
For anyone else to add to the description
Is to distort singular lives—

*

I'm not different—
You're not different—
But how we fit in has changed—
I'm transitioning from male to female—
You're switching from conservative to
Democrat—
They've just moved from suburbia to
midtown—
No one can call these changes—
My god, we just elected a crazy president!
Don't get me started!
A society on welfare
Oceans with no fish—
Nothing has changed—

The Monarchy toppled
They tell me
Because a bad harvest
Was caused by a cold winter—
Don't pin me down on the date—
If the south suffers another year of
drought

What happens to my investments!
Don't get me started!
Nothing changes—
The only certainty is change--
Nothing changes—

*

My life is normal to me
Your life is normal to you
The rapist's life is normal to him
The pusher's life is normal to him—
Why do we put red lines between us?
Until we dissolve these barriers
We'll never know how alike we are—

*

Only he who best knows himself
The wayward beast
Is able to reveal his own savagery—

*

Don't hate me—
Change what's lacking
In your life--

*

Take joy in the person
Not fear in the label—

*

We cannot think "abnormal--"
All thought is as usual—
It is easier to approach anyone
When we know we're alike—

*

Sanity is the control we allow others
To have over us—
Really the mind is subject
To no one but itself—
There is no "should", "must," "do,"
"conform—"
The mind protects itself—
The degree the mind won't yield
To the concerns of others is
Its degree of insanity—
Our minds accept us as first rank—
Everyone should be our same high
quality—

*

Life is sustained
When we surrender the promise

Of normalcy—
Life advances
Through the acceptance
Of eccentricity—

*

Clouds are innocents
Fires are innocents
All of nature is innocent
Men are innocents—
Our collective thought
Our collective action
Is less than a spot
On nature's face—
This is the way of the world
Simple and benevolent
Innocent—
We are indistinguishable grains of sand
Blowing around mighty Ozymandias--
Our lives always innocent
Of our value and effect—

*

Wounds are most vulnerable
When nearly healed—

*

The world of black and white
Ages whiter to whiter
Until it drifts off without distinction—

*

Amateurs are to be admired—
The word does mean love—
Their skills often tell us what we're
missing—
Dilettantes have reached superior
heights—
Professionals might share
Some of their respectability—

*

Art for amateurs
Mostly is happenstance and small—
Professionals can work on a largest scale
With materials requiring gargantuan
control—
Nature, with over-weening genius
Produces even more superlative results--

*

All lives are ordinary—
The boring, the endurable, the minutia

Is seen as the preponderance of them—
It is the flashes
Where consciousness and emotions respond to
Something—
These prove to be adventure, freedom
The artist beyond—
Everyday life has long roots—
From everyday growth
Is every vital fruit—

*

What do you think this world we are walking upon is!
It is art and happenstance—

*

Are professional artists challenged
By amateurs and dilettantes
Even if their talent has lifted them
To sustainable life styles?
All professions are challenged
By the uneducated and the unqualified—
If artists' lives are challenge
That is where life has lead them—

*

Every artist is a naïve explorer
Working with primitive instruments
Hands and mind—
No artist has ever been where he is
The artist at the brink
As is every person
Looking beyond what is there—

*

Some arts are just competent enough
Maybe, not quite—
But they have more heart and charm
Produced by many artists their masters—
Which would you rather have?

*

Where does the popular artist go?
Where does the classical artist go?
Back into themselves—
Where else
Deeper, is there to go?

*

We can admit
That professionals produce a greater total

Of more original and profound creations
Than amateurs who also are living longer
Like the rest of us--
But look how many professionals are remembered
For one or two masterpieces—
When someone can notice them
Amateurs can do as well—

*

Amateur art can equal the professional
In the prestigious museum—
Of course it's true—
In the world's sorry scheme
It will never be seen
It will never be known—

*

An art museum
Is the tip of an iceberg—

*

We do not have to endure dull gladly—
What no longer inspires us
Is the insipid turn-off—

All the world is replay
Until we enter it—

*

With nothing to compare it to
Our "original" art
Proves we're alive—

*

The contrast is between
The bland cliché and the familiar life
And anarchical leaps of the mind
Disrupting our isolation—
Minds sleep in indifference—
It is the startling awakening
That makes the difference--

*

Independence produces
The minimal in any art—

*

In the crusts of ordinary folks
The craziest souls rage—
So often they erupt—

But they need support
That seldom is enough—
They have but their own happiness
To sustain them—

*

To become an artist
One has to become
Other than who he is—
No wonder arts are
So wondrous and strange—

*

Wizened, gnarled, dried up
Not a breath to spare—
But from the sparest construction
A folk tune makes connection—

*

At first we had pop culture—
Then the classics came and took over—

*

If civilization advances so far
That it excludes simple love songs

It will be beyond redemption—

*

When song is lost
Nothing can take its place—

*

When did melody and heart
Get a bad name?

*

Look where the popular music is—
It's in the possession of unlearned
musicians—
Look where classical music is—
It's in the hands of MFA's
Who teach what few will listen to—
Only the individual talents
Will help their particular art survive—

*

No one listens
To artists down in their luck—
The coal mine canary

Is expected to sing
All the time—

*

If anyone says
Art is removed from life
Tell him he's a goddamned idiot—

*

Some art takes minutes or days
To pull passion from our hearts—
Some arts take an instant—
Are we to claim
One is deeper, richer than the other?

*

The artist thinks art can't be sacrificed—
The audience thinks life can't be
surrendered—
These are either/or situations—
Where we can agree to spaces
There are in-betweens--

*

Over and above wise men's exhortations
On how to live

It is obvious that even wise men fail
To live what they advocate—

*

It is only the dirt beneath our feet
But we prefer to have truth handed to us
On a silver tray—

*

Without a creative reason
Walking on our hands
Doesn't get us very far—

*

If we seriously cultured people
Aren't attuned to the "other" culture
Classical or popular
We are not cultured—
Whether seriously tuned
To esoteric jazz musicians
Or novelists who write minimally
About life under bridges
Whether block-buster movies, the top 40 hits
And ads on TV

If we are not a loose and spontaneous enjoyer
Of life
We are raw legumes
With a confused culture
We got by deprivation or turning off—

*

What is "true excellence?"
Excellence resides only within the individual—
Only the individual holds true excellence—

*

We are not driving people
Down to our level—
We have high enough opinions
Of ourselves—

*

Artists show personal intimacy
In the smallest, simplest pieces—
Technology and artifice then have less
Opportunity
To come between artist and receiver
Where weight and responsibility
Are equal and intimate—

When the intimate so often is less popular
Viewers feel they haven't got the time--
The extravagant works hit us
Like a train, brutal and one sided
Plowing into a cow—
But there it is, we value our torpor—

*

The efforts of all minds
Surely use similar energy—
By pure mechanics
Beethoven's finest effects are comparable
To the music student's Opus I—
The cashier's error returning change is similar
To an astronomer's calculations
Directing explorers to Mars—
Casual remarks will take the same energy
As a poet tossing off his verse—
Stretching for an apple
Trying one more time for a *grand jete*
Who can do more?
No one need be intimidated
No one need be diminished—

*

All thought processes are equal—
A child's struggle to understand

Two and two
Is doing what Einstein did
With MC^2—

*

Genius
Not a word we use
Has little choice
But to live alone—

*

Genius
Must encompass the world—
Originality means nothing
If millions in distance cities
Are producing the coincidental
comparable—
It is only the unique personality
That creates the original—
Only the unique causes ripples
In the world—

*

While pain might be the price
For genius to the would-be artist

That word takes on a too serious inference
With the world—

*

The concept of genius is a sop
Thrown to our egoism—
It excuses what we are unable to do
And suggests a god-given gift to a few—

We see all the time
That these geniuses fill a unique niche
That only exist
In a split moment of time—

*

The most wasting falsehood
Is that a few geniuses carry the world—
Society is the Father of Culture—
Nothing happens till the begetter falters—

*

We're much alike—
Doggedly sticking to survival mode
A transient wit
A basic understanding of rules and
propriety—

But geniuses pretty much have excluded others
And spend themselves for best effect—
And what has that to do with survival
Beyond accumulating product?
We others are modest enough—
Though also fashioned in genius
We know we're not in the line-up—

*

Who do we know of such influence
That he would speak to us?
Who are we, that others by knowing us
Can accomplish great things?

*

Farts and all
We get along pretty well
With ourselves—

*

We are all equal--
Who can we not interact with?
Who would not be rewarded to know us
As we would be to know them?

*

Part of being a genius
Is not recognizing
He leaps
From the backs of lowly seekers--

*

However we arrive at modesty
It tends to be our belief
That we don't matter—
In accepting that idea
We are giving ourselves away
To a world that has no business
Owning us—

*

If us modest people had half a chance
Just being ourselves
What a marvelous advancement
Our presence would make –

*

"True Mystic..."
How can we elevate some people
Above the character of others?
We can admit that people vary
From dabbler

To amateur
To dilettante
To artist, master
To genius
In capability and condition—
But from one to the next
Is the germ of the other—
In each is a factor of the other—

*

What vanity prepares a man
To think that classic music
Somehow surviving in manuscript
For a hundred or 300 years
Is better than a pop song
That has a good run
For ten or twenty years?
What vanity says time counts?
The rodent eaten by the cougar
Two million years ago
Had no vanity about its accomplishments
For a week, let alone for two—
Its vanity is no more apparent than ours—

*

What is the difference
Between popular and serious art
If both come from mind?

Thinking there's a value difference
between
Beethoven's and Prince's creative
processes
Will keep us on a fruitless path—
Art that begins with the elevation or
superiority
Of one over another is proof
Of privilege, profit, or prejudice—
The exception of one mental state
Over another is folly or pride—
The minds' creations, in the scheme of
things
Are so benign in their spaciousness
That evaluation is pointless--
We can do no more for ourselves
Than give thanks for all jobs well done—
Beyond that we are adding
To our own vanity and prestige—

*

The difference
Between popular and classical is
Classical takes popular
Into art techniques—
Man-hours put into art
Isn't always an enhancement—

*

It should be the creative life we value
But Prince's popular courage
Never will approach
Stout Beethoven's fictional biography—

*

Our responses to "great" art, to
"serious" art
Hardly are consistent—
An upset stomach
An over-heated hall
Fatigue
Over exposure
A restive audience—
So often our response depends
On vagaries too numerous to mention--

And how often an art gets through
The densest obstacles to stir us
In a once in a lifetime epiphany—
We have no control over an art's effects—
There is no standard way, or valid reason
To measure the worth, size, effect
Of any creative process on ourselves—

*

Grieg's piano concerto
Competing with Beethoven's "Emperor"
Wins, head over shoulders!
Or probably would
If Beethoven's name weren't attached
to his—

*

Who needs Beethoven
When the William Tell Overture is playing?

*

Does music have class barriers?
We can't say it doesn't—
It's just that we have such high regard
For our taste
We refuse to admit it's true—

*

Romantic art presents
Perfect men and woman
In moments
That are in fact
Nature's fleeting setting
Of youth--

*

Does religious music count
As proof of staunch morality
Or perhaps as commissions to pay the rent
And rewards from people of power?
An artist's passionate music
Comes of conflict and fighting the odds—
Of course he wins--
People boast of their victories
As if defeats never happened—

*

What is "Pure Music?"
We suspect it is music
No one listens to—

*

Visiting a symphony orchestra
Costs money—
Sitting in a bar with a beer in front of you
Listening to jazz is expensive
But that's the only way to enjoy music—
Internet and recordings are the cheapest connection
We have with music—
No wonder we make such distinctions
Between one kind of music and another—
All music, if it's any good

Has to be live
For it to be music—

*

A string quartet
In blue jeans—
The perfect setting
For a bus going by—

Take your pick—
A bus going by
Or a formal concern
With the man next to you
Fidgeting--

*

How do we turn
The present into the eternal?
The artist does it
Without knowing
How or why—
Art disrupts reality—

*

We derive comfort
From the classical—
We learn how to survive

With the contemporary—

*

Foolish or hesitant
We do disparage people
For being out of their time—
Have we any other option
Of being other than of our time?
We confuse the artful self
With wasteful explanations—

Genius has nothing to do with time—
Little else does either—
Only art and science seem to
And look how misguided they are--
Genius is free of time—
Genius is outside time's control—
Artists are pushed beyond their limits
When critics tag them with genius—

*

The artist
Heartily entwined
With his time
Lives the longest—

*

Art is so bound to its moment
That it is a rare art that escapes—

*

An artist is not
A lifetime ahead of himself
Or even moments ahead of his time—
He is ever himself—
If he's out of his time he is no one—
If he's not inside himself he is nowhere—

*

We cannot be praised or blamed
For being ahead of our time—
The only power an artist has
Is to connect his art and personality—
If he tries to be other than who he is
He has lost his claim to art—
Fifty years down the road
Agreeing with what was to be the future
Is empty hindsight—
A prediction, past and proven, hardly counts--

*

The only force an artist has
Is directness—
To be intricately intellectual

Usually is to be ignored—
We have a difficult time
Squaring that with Beethoven—

*

Proficient musicians are capable
Of regrettable compositions--

*

Conductors know music so well
Sometimes they think
They're qualified to compose it--

*

An artist doesn't become unique
Simply by willing it—

*

Though composers early on
May set out to write serious music
Or light music
Or popular or show or movie music
Sometimes they are mistaken
About what form they are meant to
create—
They may write their chosen for years

Sometimes successfully, sometimes
ineptly—
And sometimes they discover
What they've written they aren't fitted to
And isn't what they should be writing—
The only authentic proof of creativity
Is spontaneity—
Sometimes they are surprised to discover
That what they thought was secondary
Was the creation more to be valued—

They think they should write
What the world requires them to write—
Their numerous councilors
With their eyes on different rewards
Different careers
Think they know what's best for them—
Easy, congenial masters
Hard-driving masters
Not selected for them
Pressed upon them
When the artists were too young
To be responsible for the artists
They were expected to be—
Mr. Sullivan's serious work would be lost
Without his operettas--

Let the man present at his own birth
Decide his own path—

*

Each mind, as endless as it is
Cannot keep producing
Surprises
Unless the intelligence continues to produce
More intricate puzzles
Like a Beethoven—
This works for a while
But it too becomes cerebral sameness
And loses the passion
That set the artist on the road—

The plastic arts have a better time—
Their response comes
From the infinite variety
Of the natural world—

*

We hate to let art disappear—
We make it, rather than have it given to us—
But all things disappear—
Art will vanish
As nature wearies with all of us—

*

Oh world! Oh time!
Art dribbles through the mind
As through the neck of an hour glass
In tenuous thin line
Then disappears into the infinite—

*

If one could know
The impetus for art
And its effect
He'd capsulate the culture of the world—

*

Twenty years to a generation
Fifty years to a full creative life—
By then a life is ancient history
And close to irrelevant—
An original life is a slow creative process
Where success cannot be promised—

*

I have a bathroom—
It includes a sink, a bathtub, and a toilet—
I don't mean to astonish anyone—
But artists, most people, even
Didn't have them
A short hundred years ago--

It's a wonder they could thrive as artists
Or even be the elementary people
We'd care to associate with—
Are their accomplishments
So much more than ours"?
Can bathrooms make that great a difference?
Or is it all compromised
In convenience and sanitation?
I'm being superficial—
The curse of satisfaction?
Suffer suffer suffer
The poomph of pooping in the yard—
Now I do not exaggerate—

*

As artists go farther inside themselves
And audiences follow them
Technical skills become less important—
Certainly the knowledgeable pendulum
Of boredom is eternally swinging--
But the artist with his own interior life
Will be the one valued and discerned—

*

Police often end up with the poorest opinion
Of the people they serve—

Artists turn up their noses
At their patrons and supporters—
Aesthetes look down on the neighbors
They get their admiration from—
Gifts appear to have built-in sell-by dates--

*

When an artist crafts it
It is immediately art--
What succeeding generations do with it
Is variations on a theme—

*

Wild, bizarre, trendy
Contemporary art
Eventually succumbs
To the original and unique—
But however long it seems unbalanced
The steady reviewer keeps the best alive--

*

The notables think
They have given us the pleasure
Of their creativity—
We give them
Our precious allotted time—

*

Preferences are not comparisons—

*

In this period
Of the most museum construction ever
Some of the poorest art ever
Is being produced—

*

Any nonsense makes sense today—
Any abstruse to obtuse today
Proclaims "Anything Goes—"
No use complaining about nonsense—
The new day becomes more surreal--
Consecrated cows get the lushest pastures—

*

With all of the technical freedom today
The artist has only himself to rely on for creation—
Technology is his to do almost what he will--
Custom and tradition are hindrances
Competence is not a requisite—

The concept, the germ, the idea is the necessity—
We all have experienced competent creativity
That is acceptable at best--
We cannot know the artist's scope—
But we have been shown consistently
That the larger his project
The more constrained his freedom—
We have seen ambitious projects
That were failures
And modest creations
That have been thunderous miracles—

*

The more money needed
To produce an art
The more strained the art—
The more people involved
The more money needed—
Civic projects, movies exemplify this—
Projects become more bloated
As money becomes more the arbiter—
The project becomes a product of power
Beyond what an artist considers fruitless—
Small modest intimate products
May have been closer to an artist's inspiration—

For some the arts of the past will survive—
Reading always will survive--
But the arts that move us will come
More from local amateurs—
They wait for us to find them--

*

Art cannot do it—
It's not strong enough—
Art is a weed that thrives
Where order has been overturned—
Life, demanding most of our time and energy
Is always getting in the way
And pre-empting art's role—
Art becomes a poor cousin—

*

Museums are filled by curators
With cultures for the rich and powerful—
When a young public catches up
With those curators' generations
The lower classes will still be complaining
They have no role in it—

*

THE SIX SECOND CHOICE

I've got a secret—
One of art's many forms, painting
Is going to win the popularity contest—
Painting is the prestigious art—
It can be bought low and sold high
It can be possessed without effort
It can gain attention
Without being lost in the world's agitation--

All a painting needs is six seconds
Of actual eye contact—
And we still have the choice
Of more than six seconds if we wish—
With music, a performer or two
Or a quartet or a nonet
Or a full 100 piece orchestra
Plus a conductor
Plus us and an audience—
Fifteen minutes?
A half hour?
An opera, three and a half hours
Plus intermissions
If we're at an opera house—
In today's hectic schedules
Who's going to win?
Who lives like that?
Things to do, places to go—
Two to four hours of music a night?

Whether a screen on the wall
Or a phone in our pocket
(What do I know about those things!)
But what inspired score
Can survive constant haranguing?
Boring boring boring—
Turn it off—
Better music at the movies—
And who hears it there?

No. Paintings, six seconds of our lives—
If we can't catch it in that
Our time is better spent elsewhere—
We could try poetry—

*

Art is leveling
Even as the wealthy think
Their donations show generosity—

*

Art mostly survives in leisure
And endures in cocoons
Of peace of mind—
It is an extra, a luxury—
Appreciated, but often not explored
Deeply enough to make a difference—

*

Celebrity seldom can be accounted for
In a first month—
It should mean as little
On the thousandth day
On the seventh decade
The last day—

*

NAME RECOGNITION = MONEY = ART

*

Commercial art galleries sell
Reputation and investment—

*

The artist himself may know
He's an artist—
But most of us presume by reputation
He's an artist—

*

Art is the most prestigious way
We have of presenting ourselves
To the world—

(Money does it--)
We employ the arts
To show how unique we are—

*

Mansions
Palaces
Chateaux
Castles
Homes, habitats, condos
Must be very large—
They must have very large rooms
And even more spacious walls
For art—
Without large walls there would be few
Contemporary paintings—
Without large rooms there would be little
Music
Dance
Fashion—
Everything important
And super contemporary
Depends on extravagant living quarters—

Church and government support
Has dried up to trickles—
Art as distinct from craft
Depends on the privileged--

The arts will have to survive
Without the money of wealthy donors—
Privately subsidized art is less a solution—
Wealth always will accumulate art
Often from its own ranks—
Right now most people exist
In barren art conditions—
Art enrichment comes
When the empty cup is spilt—

*

Rich life styles come from
The poor paying for them—

*

Wealth more or less defines culture—
The lower classes pretty much
Fend for themselves—

*

The cheapest on the market
Proves to be the most expensive—

*

When you've got so much wealth
You've got to dispose of it--
Is it called generosity?

The ones receiving it
Seldom call it that—

*

Society hasn't always thought
Art is so much about nothing--
Does the trivial and inconsequential
Always conquer responsible resolve?
Must the dreadful and outrageous
Always consume our sensibilities?

*

In time
Razzle dazzle
Becomes too much in art—
One man's taste
For pomposity deadens
While another man's distain
For deep introspection shrivels—

*

There may have been no
3-D movies
Monday night football games—
They may have labored
Across rutted roads
In ox hauled carts—

But when they arrived at the cathedral
No skyscraper slouch itself
They heard the latest chorale, mass, or requiem
The same texts, the same stories
That we accept as our originals
Illustrated by light through suffused glass
Their same responses boiling
Their emotions furling to the heights—
What matter the year
What matter the culture?
It is art alive in every soul--

*

With the little we can say
About art of this time
We talk most obscurely--

*

Fashion designers invent the wheel
Every day
Flouting the traffic around them—

*

The highest skills
Seem the province
Of inaccessible people—

*

Whatever goes before
Carries a rear
Behind—

*

The art that moves us
Is the one
That is relevant to us--
We discover that it is
The artist's life
That makes it touch us—

*

Art that best expresses the artist
Makes people want to be
More a part of it—

*

THANKSGIVING CLASS

Status is measured
By the year of our Mercedes—
Status is observed
By our designer labels—

Status is promenaded
In our well-toned body
Our flawless skin
Our dentistry and our smile—
Status is defined
By the precision of our speech
The lightness of our accent
And skin—
Status seldom applies to
Freedom of self—

*

If money is your criterion
You're no better than a pig
Being pulled by a chain in its nose—

*

Whatever our circumstances
Our best guarantee of inner peace
Is our satisfaction with ourselves—

*

Anyone on a path of discovery
Welcome—
An open mind is necessary—
The world awaits an open mind—

*

We enter an art museum
And spirit envelops us—

*

Around the world
People are creating
Objects of heart-tearing beauty—
It is our duty
To be part of their risk—

*

Disreputable people
Have created sublime art
In this museum--

*

Never regret a moment
Of your life given to art--

*

After failure
We discover
Beauty
Is necessary—

*

"...no amount of money is a substitute for beauty."

T T Williams

*

The time we spend with art
Cannot be assessed—
Art is without price—

*

We walk into an art gallery
Where every painting has passed
A popularity test--
Invariably we are drawn
To those of fewest doubts—
It's all a matter of taste of course
But it is always the simple story
That pulls us more strongly to pleasure—

We visit art galleries
And are confused
By how different art is
From real life—
We do not look deeply enough—
It is all the same—

The same strangeness, originality
Startling presence
Inhabit their walls and our world—

*

Some art lets us know
Where we are—
Some art asks
Where we are going--

*

What are we supposed to take
Away from an art museum?

What have we brought?

*

Old habits are part of us—
They go everywhere with us—
Art galleries do their best
To break them up—

*

Art is for everyone--
Children visiting art museums
Are expected to find

A surprising path to discovery—
Their parents need to know
If they're not—

*

Nothing is more reassuring
Than the resolute stroke
A paint brush makes on canvas--

*

We mellow in art's mystery—
It helps us be
What we never dreamed of being--
It assuages our disappointments—

*

Dancing, painting, writing
Plowing, welding, surveying—
Art is to be lived—
Question and answer is not art—
Opaqueness and passivity are not art—
Art is not meant to weaken our lives--
Art is of no use
If it doesn't stimulate exploration—

*

Art encourages it--
Some people do their best
To appear ten years younger—
Some visitors exhibit the good taste
Of twenty years ago—
Some appear
To have their images intact—

*

You cannot wear less--
You should not wear more—
A summer lady
In a gossamer dress—

*

Social standing is lost
In an art museum—

*

We visit a memorial exhibit of an artist's works—
Some have found homes on patrons' walls—
Most never will land in museum collections--
In time some will scatter to attics, basements

And re-sale shops—
Maybe to be rediscovered
Maybe to be lost forever—

*

He was nobody, the local celebrity
Until he became famous—
Then he became interesting--

*

The gallery's almost empty—
In retrospect
A youthful portrait—
Our response makes little difference--

*

I try to avoid any composition
That's an introduction to another's work
That exalts democracy, the human worker
Or moans the terrible loss of human life
Through war, misguided gun laws,
motherhood--
When an artist works with somber purpose
He tends to trivialize--

*

With nothing to compare it to
Our "original" art
Proves we are alive--

*

An artist is one
Who thinks he can affect posterity—

*

It is admirable
And for a time it eases fear—
For a time it instills courage--
But in the long run
Art is whistling in the dark—
It changes next to nothing--

*

In the land of ancient arts
Art is always new—

*

Jazz stripped—
Zen austerity—
Live from Pompeii--

*

A painting of the pyramids
A photograph of them
A visit to them
A memory of them—
It is not a contest--

*

I am from the plains—
When ink drawings of Chinese hills
Disappearing into the mists were shown
to me
I had refused to believe them--
I should know that artists' timid imaginations
Follow actual subjects closely—
Photographs showed me this truth—
(I believed them then)
How often a blow to the head
Helps us see—

*

Beggar, street vendor, boxer
From a millennium before
Pain was among many indignities
You suffered—
Almost invisible
You were sketched in this scroll--

You were too poignant to be ignored—

*

Just by presenting the human body
As beautiful
The artist has released it
From sin—

*

Repetition has put into my brain
Between Poussin and Matisse
But a few last names--
What a place to be!

*

I'm in my Matisse paper-cutting stage—
The mechanical aids are next to go—

*

I don't paint apples—
I paint objects
Of my choosing—
Sometimes mere reddish blobs--

*

In line and color
A necklace's exquisite perfection
In a painting of a woman of culture—
She has to be beautiful
Beyond beautiful—

*

THE CLOUD WHISPERER

He's a cloud specialist
But necessarily a fickle one—
His favorite is new
Every moment—

*

Magritte saw things
We see all the time—
An egg as model
For a bird in flight--
His back reflected
By the mirror he faced—
Repetition hides singular visions
Regrettably—

*

DADA, YOUR NAME IS SIMPLICITY

*

The immediate presence
Of the new
Calling calling calling—
Every day the past becomes
Weaker—

*

It takes greater and greater effort
To appreciate the talent of the past—
Disparity becomes more distinct
More and more confusing
And less and less rewarding—

Settling into daily living
Monumental discoveries
Become inconspicuous baubles—

*

In this somber gallery
Years are stepping on
Impressionism's spritely feet—

*

Every masterpiece carries
A central idea

That insures its beauty—
It also carries a host
Of other ideas
That don't translate as well—
(It can't help being of its time)
The art of today can describe one time
Its own--

*

I walked through a museum exhibit
Of round the clock fame—
At home, alive and breathing
Away from artists' enduring brilliance
I artfully shuffled silverware--

*

Stay out of art museums—
They only show you
How short life is—

*

Another item to check off
On my holiday list:
A visit to an art store—

*

The final test of architecture is
How well it looks in ruins--

Architecture is not skeleton
Is not space refined
It is space intuited—
The whole never
Is as complete
As the fragment--

*

Missing pieces
Are the whole contained
In the beyond--

The broken leads to possibilities
The complete cannot contain--

*

The pyramids—
It's amazing
How we attach permanence
To them—

*

Often times the artist's best dreams
Are the viewer's opportunity

To explore farther
Than the artist had considered—

*

When a craftsman is in love
With his work
He is an artist of the highest caliber—

*

Whatever a person takes care and time
To craft
Has to be beautiful—

*

As long as we doubt
Our vision is not our own
That we're not seeing clearly
We never will be able to deal with others
Honestly or totally in a full-hearted way—
Whether artist, artisan, or average guy
Our independence of heart
Determines our fitness
With the world—

*

Most say it is our brains
We are in debt to—
It is our fingers
That brought us here—
Our brains have taken over
And lost the touch
They had with the natural world--
Our fingers lost touch
When they could not compete—

*

The stem and bowl of a martini glass—
Is there any reason to go on?
The knots between pearls
On a three foot long necklace
The mat and frame of an oil painting—
If you think these add a louche tone
To the discussion
The cradle of an ax and handle
The knob on a Shaker chest of drawers
The plaiting of a straw broom—
We cannot dismiss the genius
That the fingers first create—

*

The heart
Connects most intimately
To the fingers--

*

One must know the rules for craft—
But art is more than craft—
It is a passion that escapes rules--

*

"Whose is it?" asked the plutocrat
About the designer cocktail table—
"My handyman put it together for me,"
Said the billionaire
Indifferent to the fortune
Listed in his name—

*

Some of our lasting experiences
Are of those few hours we've spent
At the theater—
Art can have such power--
It can remold the heart completely—

*

The first, the first, the first—
Do you remember a first?
So few firsts are important—
So few firsts last—

So few firsts are firsts—

*

Theater is the ultimate art—
Demanded by men
Denounced by men
Demonized by men
Defended by men
And stolen from men
As stealthfully
As food from a baby—

*

Theater is the most precarious art—
A clinking box office keeps it alive—

*

Drama relies on
What no one wants to admit
The frailty of people—

*

The actor learning his script
Has no more idea where he's going
Than we do in our lives—
And he's reading a script!

*

We experience Shakespeare
As text swimming
In a golden bowl—
How tranquil and reassuring—
Then a production comes alive
As "Jaws"
Recasting our lives
And stirring us so to alarm
That we wet our pants—

*

Why is it so difficult
To take from real life
And write real stories?

*

So much art includes
The kitchen sink--
So much art depends
On tossing out
The kitchen sink--

*

Let it be--

He was a young actor
Brash and hugely successful
Years ago
When I was young—
Now we're old—
His photo
Maybe it's the only one catching him
Looking so beat and soulful—
Words demean me—
My heart goes out to him--

*

Dance
Strips us of our clothes
And demands
That we be free—

*

The body—
The more clothes we wear
The more we are removed
From normalcy—

*

Could we say
Civilization is living life
Backwards?

*

Poetry is the life-blood of a people—
When it isn’t coursing through their veins
It is running down the streets—
Attention will be paid—

*

However erudite
The printed word
Hasn’t the power
Of rampage in the street--

*

Poetry is meant for everyone—
When it’s not, its purpose is lost—
Pocketed by the gentry
It’s been out of circulation ever since--

*

The same minds that are writing
Sonnets, pantoums, and villanelles
Are destroying poetry—
Homer wrote none of those
And he’s still read by multitudes—

*

Everyone is his own receptor—
Simile and metaphor
Rime and meter don't count—
His pulse matching your pulse
Is what counts—
The poet is everyman—

*

I will clean my glasses
Before I read poetry this afternoon—
Poetry is volatile enough
Without added obfuscation—

*

Art has only one destination
Discernment--
It stays on track
With story, strong and true—

*

Technical skill is a variable
All artists command—
It is not a fixed possession
As it very well was in the past—
Now artists are going
Into themselves more frequently

While technique becomes less and less critical—

*

In any art
"Infinite possibilities"
Is too little to go on—
The senses need
Something concrete and tight
A sequence, a story—

*

Art has only one destination
Discernment--
It stays on track
With story, strong and true—

*

INFINTE VARIETY

Art of endless possibilities
Doesn't know
Where it's going
Never did
And is dumb to answers—

*

Poetry is not alchemy
Turning things into what they're not—
Poetry snares the unseen--

*

Charming, grand, touching, profound
And always flitting with triviality—
That's the trouble with poetry—
It's either not worth bothering about
Or we finally start enjoying it
And thinking it's so obvious—
Poetry ventures, poetry dares
To skirt so closely
Between the sublime and mundane
That it totters on the trite—

*

A poem starts
From a beginning
And ends wherever--
And sometimes never ends—

*

When we start a poem
We don't know
How it will end—

Life is poetry—

*

Poems are about time—
Timeless—
As if we cannot read
Fast enough
And then suddenly
It ends
And we're left
Breathlessly
Where?
Out in the middle of nowhere
Lost—
And where do we go from there?
We search for our way back
To the beginning—
It is gone—

*

The artist who boasts
He planned his creation
From first to last
Is a fraud—

*

A bird's flight is poetry—
Still water is poetry—
Silence aids immeasurably
To poetry—

*

Safety is of no account--
Poetry often breeds storm!

*

Poems are brief—
They are stars
Or they are nothing—

*

God invented stars
And sand and drops of rain—
Man invented words
More than all of those god inventions
Put together
And so powerful—
What god disposes
Will silence all of us--

*

Poetry is just a hint

Of what we've thought was inevitable--
No wonder it's not popular—
How's that again?

*

No poem
Should demand more
Than a minute's pause—
First met no poem should need
More than a minute's pondering--

*

Reaching enlightenment
Through intelligence
Is like climbing a ladder
With rubber rungs—

*

Sometimes we hardly know
What language we speak—
Sometimes we hesitate to utter a word—
Sometimes we attempt borrowing
language
That doesn't work—
We still need translation
And who bothers!
Often we never find a language

For saying who we are—

*

Asked for our reason
We discover so often
If we aren't insulted
To give our reason
That the reason
For our reason
Isn't reason—

*

Ultimately
Life is poetry—
Everything is pertinent
Everything has meaning
Nothing is outside it—

*

We may think there's nothing there
But all the while it's everywhere--

*

Oh, I long to be
The wind and the rain—
One day to the next

I am who does not know
Who he is—

*

We transcend who we are
Without knowing who we are—

*

Of course it's poetry!
It's truth
Of the moment!

*

A questioning heart is poetry—

*

If the heart is true
The words are true—
Truth always replies
As poetry—

*

What is mind
Free of itself?
Poetry—

*

Poetry is no more a dodo
Than dada is abstract
Than the mind is absurd—
The mind is a false compass--
It is orderly and logical
But seems to verge
On disorder and perversity—

*

How dare we say
What poetry is!
It is not Phoenix
It is not a weed refusing to die—
It is something written from within
That won't crumble when exposed
To the world—
Better perhaps it is written
By someone who refuses to recognize
What poetry is—

*

THIS IS A TEST

Crisp crunchy crackers
Crisp soda crackers

Crisp crunchy crumbling crackling
Crunched on
Desiccated soda crackers
Choking on crotchety
Soda crackers--

*

        Disappear into
                Disappear into
Disappear into
What a perfect New Year's Eve poem—

                Reaching out
What a perfect New Year's Day poem--

*

NEXT   BE   ST
    THIN   G   TO   FREE

*

I do not put messages in bottles—
I put notes in books—
What love is glowing
What radiance flowing—
Have you found them yet?

*

Of course my poems are precious!
When you're writing of the moment
Everything is precious--

*

I suffered a million mosquito bites
This evening—
I exaggerate—
Maybe two or three—
Discomfort never meets its match--
Mild irritation—
The foretaste of trouble to come--
My mosquito allies prepare my way
In the world—

*

This is my heart—
It is the infinite sky
Scattering clouds—
This is my heart—
I am a drop of rain
Dripping from a bold leaf—
I can never die—
I am a part of you—
I am everywhere—
Hear me, feel me beating—
I am beating within you

Forever--`

*

I turn the pages, poem by poem
Of a poet of so long ago—
I feel I am brushing his hands—
Know I am reaching out for you—

*

Throw away the book--
I want your living heart—

*

A poet is of little influence
With his poetry alone—
He must twist inside you
With every mode of art
Including living—

*

My sensitivity
Without question
Is equal
To the Zen Masters—
I need to prove it?
Your sensitivity

Marches with Shakespeare's—
No dispute—

*

SU'LUK = outcast poet who roams alone

*

Creativity is a spark—
Without tinder
It soon will die—

*

If we could begin to see
We could not write
It all down—
Poets are rare--
They see a little
Of the something
We all miss—

*

My valley is dark and deep
And lonely—
There you stand
On the crest
Strong and green

With roots sunk deep
With not a leaf
Blowing my way—

*

The poet, old and bent
Unsure of footing—
Crackling doesn't matter—
His words go out
Beyond hearing—

*

The world's parade is recorded
In the rows of poetry books
Monumentally gathering on my shelf--
More than likely to be dispensed with
Or buried in a landfill—
That's the way of the world—
Lucky animals
Without our history of farce and tragedy!
I would laugh
But I'm close to crying
That so many poems are left
Unread—

*

The poetry in the daily news

Would fill a poetry library—
The poetry in a poetry library
Might fill a shelf
In a poetry sanctuary—

*

We have read these many years—
All these hours
Come to a lifetime—
What is a lifetime after all?

*

It is difficult to trust advice
When it is given
With a seeming lack of wisdom—
When everyone knows what we know
It is difficult to be convinced
They can help us in any way—
The truth is
We pretty much know
What everyone else knows—
But it comes to each of us
So jumbled in emotion
That it is brand new and unnerving--

*

The advice of the wisest seer

And the dumbest oaf vary little—
Each is giving what would be best for
himself--
And what has that to do with you?
Advice is nothing without poetry—
Poetry opens the door
Where perception is held prisoner—

*

A Rumi-ism is hardly any good
Until it is translated into poetry
And free to do its work—

*

Listen to the wise, saying
"Only the wise shall save us—"
What fool said that!

*

When they run out of things to do
Let the wise men decide who is wise—

*

Dogs sniff
At other dogs' asses—
This conventional formality

Must tell them something about those dogs—
Shit must have its distinctive properties--
Maybe no, maybe yes—

People sniff—
They ask questions--
Maybe answers are distinctive--
Maybe no, maybe yes—
"How much did that cost?"
"Where do you live?"
"What school did you go to?"
Innocent questions with unclear answers—
Maybe no, maybe yes—
Sniff sniff—

*

UPON EXAMINATION

When the Greeks and the Renaissance
Discovered the wonder of men
We can forgive their pride—
Now we can say they over did it—
There's nothing wonderful about men—
We've seen enough of them
To have a different opinion--
They're only the long end
Of a continuing temporary line of life
And the only unique thing about them

Is that they are expressive about
mortality—
Such a wonder—
Maybe--
We could say that death gave us heart--
Maybe--
That gives us a modestly sad difference—

*

We don't respect differences—
We expect the world to be the same
as us—

*

A piece of work is man?
We're so full of ourselves
We've almost disengaged ourselves
From the world!
However much we try to think
Of softening "dominion"
Per god's instruction
We're still dominating and destroying—
When the earth returns to itself
There will be no sign of man
And god will be content
To be his eternal selflessness—

*

We need not worry about the world—
It will get along without us—
And better for all the good we want to do—

*

The horizon lies low
Obedient and at rest—
We don't see
Its open wounds
Those wide gashes cut through
And plateaus wasted in every breathing pore—
The earth lies still—
It will collapse
And take us with it—
The earth will come back without us
And be as beautiful as before—

*

Read this book of poems
Slowly—
I would like to think you were pausing
Where I slowed down for reflection—

*

I created this

By noticing it—

*

I've often thought I should be
A stone mason—
All the rocks I've piled
And pavers I've placed—
I'm still at it
Sweeping grains of sand
Endless grains of sand—

*

It comes somewhere in life—
To artists it comes early and strong--
It means value outside of life—
It means life out of balance—
It means looking for life within—

*

It is enough to write in obscurity
If he writes in abundance and earnestness
About his times—
However lopsided his ideas
If he is of his time
Agitated
Or moving gracefully in his milieu
He will command authority--

No one else is able
To produce his exactness of time—

*

The poet's lines become
An unsteady support
To the reader's ready life—

*

Words have more meaning
When we are young
And don't understand their import—

*

I write all the time—
I tell no tales—
People don't figure into my words?
What the hell do you think
I'm writing about!

*

With basic vocabulary
I put down lines
That can't be understood--

*

The more words used
The more meaning totters
In abeyance—

*

As a poetry reader
I get very nervous—
The least little bit
Foreign to the poem
Trips me up—

*

Calling things into being
With words
Is creating fantasies—
Names only create non-existence—
Words have no truth—
We must live with a minimum of words
If we are to live truthfully—

*

My language
Is one no one else speaks—
You think you understand me—
Why are we arguing?

*

I seized every strategy
Used every wile
Braced time against sleep—
With ever fatuous excuse
I wasted all the time I could
And still
Completed my procrustean writing—
The goal was more compelling
Than the obstacles—

*

I am an ineffectual artist—
Most inefficient—
But I create—

*

Goodbye, button-down world, goodbye—
What comes is connecting dots
That I finally see—
There have been more subtle signs
Internal and harder to ignore
More dangerous
Certainly more harmful to good health—
But ignoring, procrastinating
Is a universal habit
Mine too particularly—

Goodbye, world
The setting is opportune—
No doubt no more advantageous
Than any other—
If anyone would wait
For my defense--

*

I'm a little doubtful about my direction—
Goodbye, world, not as good riddance—
What took me so long?

*

Revision upon revision
Cloud layer upon dotted clouds
Upon clouds
Smudged, incoherent, contrary--
Order out of disorder
Out of disorder—

*

Of course craft and revision
Follow an original design—
Like a key that opens the occult
They make for comfortable and
acceptable—
But unrestrained revision muddles

The original creation—

*

THE BUS STOPS HERE

*

Waiting for the bus—
Every texture and twig
On the sidewalk
Reveals its identity—

*

We are united by blood
We are united by tears
We are united by poetry—

We are united by dirt
We are united by grief
We are united by poetry—

We are united by clouds
We are united by mountains and plains
We are united by poetry—

We are united by kindness
We blessed in love
Poetry all--

*

The poet recited the word "love"—
He lived it
He didn't have to repeat it—

*

Love is sensing another's need
That you must fill--

*

Give them no other choice
But to be nice to you—

*

Honestly
Has anyone ever considered
Sending poetry out
For extra-terrestrial contact?

*

If it's for poetry
The poet finds where to read—
If it's for society
The group manages to ring up a poet

Who fits—

*

I used to be all dichotomies inside—
Now I'm all one and the same—

*

We wear masks for people—
They don't make any difference—
No one knows us—
Why our disguises?

*

It is not for me to figure me out—
It is for you to make sense of me—

*

An artist writing for approval
Is embedded in quicksand—

*

At the end of the day
Down to essentials--
My notebook and a pen—

*

Hours with strangers, unknowns
And lifelong friends—
An idle afternoon with words—

*

A bridge too far—
Time for another
Glass of wine—

*

A glass can hold no more wine
Than it's designed to carry
But it does—

*

I tap my wine glass
For its mellow tone—
If I were a musician
I'd recognize the tone
And its meaning—
As it is
I just keep drinking—

*

"Eat, drink, and be merry—"
God created man
To exploit that phrase—

*

Glass inside glass
Worlds inside worlds
Seen, not seen
And multiplying the impossible—

*

Glass cannot conceal
Its imperfections—
Insubstantial as we are
Our lives ought to be guided
As freely--

*

The intoxication of poetry—
No, the intoxication of wine—
They should never be taken together
The pure heart of poetry
And the veering brain of wine--
They shouldn't be used together?
Poetry or wine
Wine or poetry
I don't know which is which—

How can they not be mixed
When they're a mix of one?
Wine and poetry are one—
Drink, drink
Drink to me only with thine eyes
Drink, drink, drink—

*

Some say
Reality is as intoxicating as wine—
Why not both?
Oh the suspense, the danger
For the moment!
Alcohol seeks to ensnare
An undiscoverable identity—

*

Life too often
Is the expectation of an olive
At the bottom of a martini—
No goal should be so overblown!

*

As I drink champagne
From a plastic flute
With baroque swirls, prisms, bands
Borrowed from finest crystal

Real and fake unite in liberal cause--

*

Better than pouring
One's own champagne—
A lover or servant?
One and the same—

*

Opening a new bottle—
Gold at my fingertips—
Champagne at my lips—

*

I accept gold—
It doesn't have to be real
It doesn't have to be abundant—
It can be scattered like leaf
It can be tinsel
As long as it glitters—
Best of all
When it circles the nose
Of a champagne bottle—
Champagne—
And all wrapped in gold—

*

You don’t know me—
You don’t have to know me—
Listen to my words—
You need no more—
What someone says about me
About my words
Aren’t me—
It is my words
That should mean something
Or nothing to you—

*

How would he know my story?
Not because I’m unique in any way—
But because my awareness
Of the ordinary has made it so—

*

How is a person “unique”
And an artist?
How is he timeless?
By being explicitly within himself—

If our efforts are clear
To others
We’re probably aware
Of our closeness to ourselves--

*

My books are
An improvisatory art—
I change, make up, revise
As I go—

*

You're lucky
When you're alone
To find a way into yourself--

*

Dickinson had me with death and daffodils—
She lost me with sugary robins and bees—
Uncommon sweetness nudged us apart—
We met in common ignorance--
Me with phases of the moon
Her with passages toward death—
She goes on—
I take relief—

Emily Dickinson
Enjoy your sentiment—
If an old maid, likely women for friends
Use your spinsterhood frugally—

Be a poet—
So much more satisfactory
Than a warm body next to you in the night
An awkward body poking and
provoking you—

Poetry provides our best options—
Our little tiny notebooks
Like a woman sewn together
After Caesarian birth
We have our tiny notebooks--
Even those are inflammatory—

*

Everyone amasses his mountain
differently—
Mine is tiny notebooks
Numbering through hundreds—
As mountains they're not much—
I don't pretend they are—
But they're mine—
Words, unaccounted for
In a random heap—

*

What's your mountain?
However it contrasts with mine
It is a mountain--

*

A poem can be like
Something slow and organic
Or off the top of the head
Like a Zeus' Minerva—

I'm in an anti-mood—
So much for creativity
So much for truth—
Poetry and truth, or truth?
I'm stretched in different ways—

*

THE SUPREME COURT

Imagine a Federal Judge
Whose opinions are so well crafted
Even if askew
That general readers follow them
For pleasure and instruction--
And further
That when physicists and painters
Write with precision and charm
Biologists, farmers, poets harvest their
thoughts
In profit and delight--
To discover such reward in words

Avid and desultory readers
Scan volumes for these treasures—

Philosophers, writers, let felicity and vigor
Brighten your words--
Write them with verve--
Don't give anyone an excuse
To tune you out--
Insure that every reader
Whatever his background
Becomes hooked on your words
And makes an exuberant occasion of it--
The reader's new found pleasure
Is charged with such energy
It carries him and society positively
forward—

*

We discover that another's amiable culture
Is stirring to so many people—
How can all the world not be of prime
interest
To all of us?
Wooed by the seductive world
How can we not want to rush into the arms
Of beguiling authors and say
"Lover, you have captured me—
Let us ravish each other totally—"
This taste of excellence is like

Piercing the smooth skin
Of a luscious fruit—
The warmth, the aroma
Fully excites our expectations
And the flesh drips freely and abundantly
Onto our hands and into our mouths—

This reward expands
As easily an exotic jungle movie when a key
Fits into the monumental skull
And the door to vast treasure slides open—
The quest for total adventure begins
All over again—

A glorious phrase
Not written down
And forgotten
Never is retrieved—
Rare, recherché, inimitable—
What do we miss
When we try to reconstruct the ensemble?
It is gone forever
To become the stuffed resemblance of a
flying bird—

*

APPROXIMATE

We're almost certain it's not the right
word—
Approximate—
We all know situations
Where approximate is okay
Even if we know it's miles apart
From what we meant—
Approximate—
Fitting together, like a simile—
Did they fit tighter than that?
Is that what we meant?
Weren't we more precise?
Approximate--

But how are we assured
That what we read is accurate?
What gives it the authority
When we know so much knowledge
Is garbled?
The "facts" of the world are so vast
That exploitable knowledge
Is the accepted condition—
We never will exhaust the source
Of knowledge—
It will always be the well
That never runs dry—
Witnessing an event is the surest way—
But as much to the point
A reputation of integrity and inclusiveness
Is our assurance of dependability--

Let us enjoy words first as
entertainments--
When being accepted as facts
Let us ask what references apply—
Language flows easily—
The author and the idea are so
completely one
So naturally a part of each other
That the ideas, smooth and steady
Are without doubt or excess--
Like a field of grass in the wind
Standing fluid and responsive to every
force—
Facts so common
We don't recognize all of them—
We discover nothing special about them
Where the vital spark resides—

At present we are gleaners
Scratched and scarred drudges
Catching every burr
Thinking vainly
That ideas are hidden and hard to
come by—
Ideas should be as easy as walking
Through a field of heavy bending grasses
And catching every seed—

*

I know nothing about law—
I know nothing about drugs—
But when a gentle, humane country
Waffles between law and benevolence
I back humanity—
The best of lacking love
Is worse
Than muddling through
With love—

*

"I know"
Is the best way
To be lost in the shuffle—

*

Open open open—
A closed mind is close to dead
If not dead—
Open!
What do you have to lose?
If you have a change of mind
What is that to you?
You still have control of yourself—
You can stop—
You can go back—
You can proceed cautiously

Or exuberantly
To a new future—
Nothing is ordained
Nothing is contrary to your abilities—
You are still you--
And maybe for being more open
Maybe more alive—

*

If one is closed to receiving
He is incapable of learning—
He is performing by rote—
Learning is as simple as receiving—
Learning need not be threatening—
If its intention is good—

*

That our personal power extends
Beyond ourselves is illusion—
We can acknowledge, grant, or confer
Powers beyond ourselves
But we do that only by agreeing
That they are temporary and borrowed—
They are never owned, or achieved—
Our values, except as suggestions
Must be controlled within each one of us--

*

Dynamite is nothing
Until some spark ignites it—
Power is nothing
Until some passion provokes it—
The world is benign
Until an opportunity opens it
A stimulus lifts it—
We might know
That opportunity is there
All the time—
We might make sure
We do not waste it
On destructive self-defeat—

*

Astonishing stories flash
From the newspapers all the time—
So many
That the absurdities melt
Into the ordinary—

*

Virtue is nothing
Until it accepts its darker side
As part of its being—

*

Virtue that expects reward
Is no virtue—
Virtue oblivious to reward
Is love—

*

If moral art
Can't hold its own with ordure
Why would we value it?
If art tries to prove
Ordure diminishes us
Why would we respect it?

*

A yes or a no
In moral judgment
Make us think
We know more
Than the world does--

*

Judging reduces—
Loving increases—
Justice might seem the goal
But love must prevail--

*

Judgment implies knowledge—
What makes you think you know
Everything?

*

When we judge someone
By a single incident
Is it him or us?

*

Truth is a word little used
In polite society--

*

Reading begins in our childhoods
When we are soft and secure in love—
Reading and thinking, from love—

*

Reading is pleasure—
Pleasure is learning—
Learning is reading—

*

What pure strains
Are they coming from?
What are we doing
When we add truth to truth?

*

If writers of Letters to the Editor
Stuck to facts they know from experience
What a wonderful world this would be—

*

No thought is too small
To be epic—

*

Don't get too big for yourself—
Don't let education go to your head--

*

Knowing
Is not the same
As being able
To do it—
We do not know
Until we are able to do—

*

A lifetime of words
Doesn't mean
We've learned something—

*

Whatever the simple answer
There's always a simpler one—

*

The simplest explanation
With the fewest words
Is the best reply—
That guarantees our ego
Won't become involved—
*

Truth is like describing
A highway's landscape
At one point
And then at another point
A thousand miles away
As the exact same road—

*

When the mind is active
Everything is relative to it
Everything is available to be received—
Everything is connected
And of supreme and equal importance—
This does not mean distraction
Endless loss in endless flutter—
We still have presiding interests and goals—
But with everything always beckoning
The world is rich beyond lacking—

*

Willfully perverse
Or woefully stupid—
No one's publisher
In particular—

*

We prove our quality
By reaching for a book--
Porn, page turner, whatever—
They can be so lost in our activity
They don't mean much—

*

Books are strangers first—

Do you remember
How you met?
Were you introduced
By well-meaning friends?
Did you read of its reputation?
Did you hit it off immediately?
Tolerate each other?
Skim, really get into it?
Did you pretend it was more serious
And quickly decide to meet again?
Was it a mad relationship
Swaying in and out of love
A page, a chapter, an evening at a time?
Books are relationships—

*

The word—
The spoken word—
Not as it is written down
Not as it is recorded—
Not as it is painted
On wall, on canvas
Carved in rock, lifted on lintel and cornice
Not as it is filmed, encapsulated
Not as it is noted in a score—
The word
Freely spoken
Sung
Danced

The word
Of the moment
To be free
And then vanish
Forever—

*

MUSIC IS THE ONLY VERITY

*

Put your glasses aside—
Any variation of vision works
For music--

*

A violin can move mountains—

*

Sound--
You had to be there—

Sound--
Being there, the only art—

*

Imagine that hollow empty place
Where nothing is heard—
The place of all melody
Silence—

*

An aria opens
Like a new leaf on a tree
Like a mother presenting her baby to its father
Like a rainbow after weeks of rain—
As much goes into a singer's high C
As a lover finding his long sought love—
The high C is our miracle--
Open, enfold us
Lift us, fly away with us
Let us drift
To fall as every leaf will fall—

*

MUSIC IS EMPOWERMENT

*

In the somber cathedral
The holiness of musicians
In rehearsal
Talking about the conduct

Of their performance—

*

No one has concluded
That god is pure melody—
Haunting and heart breaking
Vigorous and strong
No line separating
No meaning obscure
Probably all sound merges
In god's heavenly choir—
Where is one beauty and another?
Formula and melody connected
One one one—

*

The music sails on--
It is heard throughout the world—
The birds catch it
Take wind, and sing—
God raises the breezes
And rustles the leaves—
The concert ends
But the music goes on
Forever—

*

LOFTY PLACES

The stones absorb the music—
They grow
Taller and taller—
Look how they climb—
What is feeding them?
What are they drinking?
The music!
Enough!
They cannot grow any higher—
The stones, the music—
Without contest
They feed on each other—
Stone hearts melt
Solid stones stretch and bend—
Stone and music—
Forming arches
Admitting light--
They soar
Taking our hearts with them—

*

The formalism
Of an empty concert stage
Before the passion begins—

*

Oh to be free!
I am freed!
Music—

*

It's summer!
Attend as many free concerts
As you can!

*

Babies crawling
On the concert's summer lawn—
Grass never will be so honored—

*

Attaining old age
We arrive at concerts
Strong in heart--

*

The heart is melody—
Without heart there is no melody—
If it is not melody it is not heart—

*

Music can be spirit and soul-searching
And rise out of tragedy and remorse—
We know about its restorative powers—
Music is the best escape from care
And the best for ritual remembrance—

*

Especially dancing
Especially marching
Especially feet tapping
Our body twisting
Our arms raising--
The New Glory, music--

*

Music, because we dare not endure
Words escaping out of control—

*

Music is adding nothing to my psyche—
It is pushing for
Large empty spaces to be filled--

*

Classical music documented
The established and the ideal—

Romantic music had to explode
What wasn't so—

*

Classical music attempted
To maintain the status quo
But along came Beethoven
With manuscript markings bristling
To sweep away the cobwebs—

*

The charm of old music
Is that it can seem
Strange to educated ears—

*

Classical music relies on balance
To prepare us for what is coming—
Classical art is familiarity
And constriction—
Rhythm, meter, repetition
Give it stability—

The farther we go from the classical
The deeper we go into the unknown—
Less anticipation, more suspense,
surprise—

Longer melodic line--
Our composure
Of seeming artlessness
Sustained with less structured thought
And more exotic experience—

*

The classicists weren't worried
By long lyric lines
As much as they were about "form—"
Inspiration wasn't song
As much as it was balanced structure—
Beethoven, apparently in mid-air
(What a place to be)
Was on a trajectory
With no support on either side--
He was no where
Free of references--
The soon-to-be Romantics
Thought they saw safety in his leap
And followed—

*

Paper provides proof of the prejudices
we are--
Classical was straining outside itself
Re-shaping oratorio into opera

Forcing measured bars into darkening tempests—
Beethoven couldn't have given a shit—
Few write like him any more
Or need to—

*

Music is a foreign language
Which everyone seems to understand
But clearly needs to be taught—

*

Technical skill is a variable
All artists command—
It is not a fixed possession
As it very well was in the past—
Now artists are going
Into themselves more frequently
While technique becomes less and less critical—

Can we classify artists
As exterior or interior artists?
Presently we're valuing
The interior artist more
The Beethovens, the Debussys—
The exteriors probably would be
Haydn, St. Saens—

The superior techniques
Of a Bach or Mozart
Certainly carry them along—
The ravishing beauties
Of a Tchaikovsky, Puccini, Ravel
Perversely make technique dismissive—
Though these interior artists
The ones that demand most
Of an audience's attention
Now are the ones we prize the most--
The danger is
They can go so deep
Into obscure personality
That contact is lost—

*

Every age unwittingly
Escapes its time—
Its known convention is pressing
Pushing to break out of itself—
Oh art!
What does it want to say?
Why isn't an artist's vocabulary ever
enough!
"I wish, I want, I must—"
But what is he trying to do?
To free himself
To arrive where no man ever has been
Free free free--

*

Dies Irae, Dies Irae
Repeat it often enough
And it loses its danger—
It is a comfort and a pleasure—
Consorting with a fugue and variations
Music and a glass of wine
Repeat it, repeat it
Dies Irae, over and over
Music and a glass of wine
Over and over
Pleasure and a wine glass
Music and Dies Irae—

*

Plink, plink, refined music—
Any music can be reduced
To basic components—

*

Listen to him!
He creates worlds
By putting dots on paper—
We can travel anywhere with him—
A poet is lashed to lines
That have to mean something--

*

Some art
Is for the body's delight—
Haydn's goal—
Some art
Tantalizes the mind—
Some art
Satisfies the soul—
The body demands all—

*

GETTING BY WITH LESS

Haydn spent three decades composing
For his patron, the noble Esterhazy—
Imagine the stability
Imagine the constant flurry of fashion
And the likely stress
That security might come to a cleaver
ending—

"How long have you been working for us?
"Haydn, you're so well thought of
You're like family, if in livery—

Sonatas, trios and quartets
Full symphonies, masses, and operas—

"What symphony, was it 17 or 18
When you started with us?
I wish I could have given you a timpanist
But the horses have been going through shoes
Faster than our need for a musician--
And you have such a good way
Of getting by with less—
Your patience and virtue
Are appreciated exceedingly—"

Those lucky Esterhazys
That fortunate Haydn
We blessed ones of future times—

*

Well, Haydn, what did they expect from him?
Hardly music for tomorrow!
To bring wood in for the fire?
Yes, he certainly expected
To do that too—

*

Haydn
Through all his servitude
Entertained—
When finally free

He entertained--

*

FOOTBALL AND ART'S TRAUMA

Haydn never played football—
Every family that glories in it
Handles its violence differently—
Its violence means little to me—
I'll never lose a son to the game—
Let them bask in the excitement
In the brawn, the mayhem, the sex
The power, the nobility—
When injury eliminates the young and hardy
Families feel both united and torn apart—
Let them call the game what they will—
I've never heard of a Haydn quartet
Affecting families like that
But I know it could happen--

*

Haydn stuck to the rules--

*

Haydn was into mundane matters

Like putting his musicians on coaches for family leave—
Wagner was into ritual, myth, and interstellar travel—
The world was more important to him—
Art suffers when world conditions
Are more important than people suffering--

*

Haydn, you modest beautiful person—
It's time to put your symphonies in order—
87 before 85, 86 before 84
And 85, most popular, taken out of third place
And put first—

I'm confused—
Haydn, maybe you're not--
Numbers being immaterial
Each is your favorite child—
Maybe like my numbered and dated notebooks
Maybe like Dickinson's stitched chapbooks—
Compatible company, I flatter myself—
We modestly persist
And in our quiet ways get lost
In superficial numbers—

*

So many of Haydn's symphonies
Have affectionate titles—
Cunning music
How charming, how bogus—
But how better to win fans
Than with familiarity and kinship?
Besides, Haydn didn't name them himself—
Did Beethoven name his sixth
Or his seventh or eighth?

*

Everyone needs balance—
Haydn is a hinge—
Haydn helps keep us sane—

*

Haydn was an "entertainer absolute"
In his day—
He was a gifted musician—
Music can age better than wine—

*

Haydn knew the reason for art—
His was the sparkle in the wine--

Entertainment—
Everything else was incidental—

*

Haydn, even when he thought of it
Was unable to make himself over
To be adaptable and current--
Modest man—
Someone had the opportunity
To see his worth and give him
independence—

*

I was in the audience that exclaimed
"Haydn, come to London, come to
London—
Make your presence known—
Give your music to the world—"

*

Beethoven and Haydn?
No comparison—
They had different parents—

A difference between them might be
Beethoven is admirable for his music—
Haydn is loveable—

Does that make a difference?
Character makes the difference—

*

A man tired of Haydn
Is tired of the world—

*

Mozart lived a life of peril
But oh the sweetness and the light—
He sent out alarms
But no one heard them—
As usual
No one understood or cared—

*

What can we say
When we are dying?
With death lurking
Mozart wrote three symphonies—
We wish he could have written more—

*

Mozart expresses mystery—
Bach brings in the sublime—
Beethoven amasses struggle and defiance

And in hauteur defines music his way—
That gruff old stuff goes a long way—

*

If I hear one more pianist
Or over-the-hill musicologist lament
How easy it was as a youth to play Mozart
And now how infernally impossible it is
In maturity to measure up to him
I'll rudely rage at his funeral—
It's bad enough that we deify a man
Who composed perfectly in his head
But at least we can admit
That as he reached growing maturity
He faced and missed deadlines
Fought with patrons and impresarios
And battled temperamental singers—

Notes as written
Finally have to carry some of the weight—
Wouldn't it be possible to play them
With respectful technical skill
And come out with an admirable
performance?

And what about Haydn?
We hear very little about soul in his
music—
Do musicians pass him off

As deserving no better than perfunctory?
Let's give performers' explorations a rest—
Art survives
When a musician plays notes for a
listener—

*

No art has the league of boosters
music has—
Arts seldom are as honored and elevated—
Even musicians think themselves godlike
And are vocal in self-praise—

*

Is a minor composer
To be dealt less considerately with
Than a Beethoven?
Would any responsible musician save
himself
For Beethoven
And play a lesser composer carelessly
Does a carelessly played Beethoven
Sound worse
Than an ineptly played second rater?
Can any composer expect his music
To be heard as he wrote it?

*

Music is hand-woven carpets—
Haydn crafted carpets
Upon which furniture sits
And children play—
Beethoven knotted rugs of intricate design—
Mozart embellished rugs that fly--

*

Chopin is a garden
So full of blossoms
Any others are not missed—

*

Do I think less of Mendelssohn's music
Because of his happy, trouble-free childhood?
Would his music mean more to me
If he had been miserable and a monster
Maybe disappointingly human?
I slight him for his unrealized self
For merely being himself--

*

TRAGIC OVERTURE

Being a romantic
Possessing an orchestra
Brahms thought tragedy
Was an intellectual exercise—

*

A lizard stationed itself
To hear the voices singing
In the garden--
If I choose to believe
That a lizard enjoys choral music
No one is lessened by that—

*

A lizard makes its way
Through a maze of blooming lily spears—
Heaven is not always
What it is made out to be—

*

The music grows more sustained
Slows and almost stops—
Can music stop?
It hovers without motion
Without increase or diminuendo
On a breathless summer day—
Without direction

Without elevation—
Music, as substantial
As a firefly at dusk—

*

Music out of nothing
The tornado on the prairie
A power not to be ignored—
Without accounting
The intimate and subtle melts
The hardened heart—

*

Somewhere in dark space
Is a void
Where aria floats like cosmic dust--
These sounds, these heart-wrenching songs
Wrap us in their fragile bounds
And lift us to where we began—

*****

BEETHOVEN

What's to suffer?
We suffer--
Why are we forever attempting
To find reason for suffering?
What's to be made of it?
We who want to survive
In spite of everything?
Reason is beside the point—
We suffer because we suffer--
Suffering is part of life—
We suffer—

The effect of that suffering
Often is up to us—
Some of us end miserably
And cause no end of suffering to others--
Some of us maintain minimal lives—
Some of us end as craftsmen in wood
Delivering carbonated beverages
Cutting grass and hedges
Selling stocks and bonds—

Some of us survive humanely
Some of us endure--
Some of us triumph—

*

While pain might be a price
For genius

It is not only to an artist
That it matters--

*

Pain
Is the destruction
And the refiner
Of character—

*

Disability can enhance spirituality—
But spirituality is a survival jewel
Brightest when worn modestly—

*

If we have to have been hurt
To know what hurt is like
We can't begin to heal
Until we help another heal—

*

Beethoven was the unique misfit—
He was brilliantly intelligent
And an astonishingly abused egoist—
He reveled in them, and then suffered
Increasing deafness—

Imagine a ruined virtuoso career—
He would show them!
He'd put all that brilliance into composition—
Further and further out of the music realm—
Humanity showed up
In the seriousness of his quest—
The abstractness of music
Is the best thing going for it—
He wasn't a total monster—
Humanity was discerned in him—
Imagine that—
But always arrogant
Always the put-upon
Shaking his fist even at death—

*

If god had wanted to "punish" Beethoven
He'd have given him adequate hearing
And abundant health
And left him
The superficial, deplorable man
He seemed destined to be—

*

What does Beethoven have to complain about?

Deafness forced him to change course—
He might otherwise have been forgotten
As a blustering ill-tempered improviser
Instead of honored
As a searching soulful genius—

*

Beethoven personifies
The secular tragic life—
There is nothing tragic about it—
The world does not bestow tragedy
On anyone--
The world is too remotely oblivious
For that—
With artful industriousness
We go about defining tragedy
To assuage our high flown dignity--
Oh how he suffered!
The beauty is
His awareness made it count—
The composer he wasn't
As a callow youth
And might never have become
Was uprooted by the affliction
That drove him to reach—

*

Suffering can be ennobling

When we can hope for an end to it—
What we do with it is up to us—
We can learn from it
And be more loving persons
And say suffering has been conquered—
For many people suffering
Is but a far off continuance of it—
The poor are helped little
And seldom have the means to end it—
Often it compounds in misery—
From those who have little
Much is taken--

*

We argue that none of us, the competent
Is completely in control of his life—
None of us is—
And none of us face
The exact conditions
That anyone else does--
Our gratitude goes out
To the man, somewhat sharing our complexity
Who can throw us a bone of great art—

We argue that the less stellar of us
Are less challenged than the geniuses
And thus have less character challenges
To heighten our talents--

Our proof is the uplift we get
From those bones
Of great art cast to us
That we so greatly appreciate—

*

DIGNITY IS A ONE PERSON ATTITUDE

*

We'll never know
How ease or trial affect
An artist's career—
It's so much to conjecture
That it's pointless to consider--

*

There we were
Nice intelligent young children
Sweet little girls or boys
Embraced and loved
Until all that was secure
Family, the familiar, approval
Was torn from us--
And it was those miserables
Who were conscripted to coddle
Us others who needed help—

*

Whatever our family's standing
We and our parents always are novices
To the game we're in—

*

Children grow up
On heart—
They respond to intelligence
But their most substantial food
Is heart—

*

Every time a relation
Abuses his child
Society shares the blame—

*

It is mere banality to say
The world produced a Beethoven
And every unexceptional one of us too—
Were it not for every extraordinary
happening
In our lives
We would not, could not be
Who we are—

No one particular thing
Makes us captains of our lives--
We respond as we are influenced—
Circumstances
Have mated us perfectly
To who we are—
We have no one to be
Other than who we are—
This is so obvious--
We are roiled in singular events
All our extraordinary lives--
As we try self-improvement
We face little likelihood for change--
We are formed thus--
If we take prescient moves
At critical moments in our lives
They are mostly accidents—
Most of our decisions
About changing our futures
Are vapid wishes--

What is our originality?
It is in every variation in the air—
Where is our creativity?
It is in every spanking
In every harsh word, promise of love
Assurance of support
That our parents gave us budding
youngsters—
Where is our passion?

We think it comes from our hearts and souls—
It comes from every chemical
Real or placebo
That are mixed in universal test tubes
Without formulas of time and volume
That create every one of us
Unique and new--
With that, in mild conformity
Or in struggle and burning
We try to be more than we are
As we stave off death—

*

Often enough it is
A single crucial moment
We never were aware of
That sets the tone
Of an unendurable and complicated life—

*

Comparisons are worthless—
We do not need Disney-destructive
Super-villain parents
To ruin our childhoods—
The unnoticed and hardly perceived actions
That we endure every day
Are as disastrous

As gunshots to the body—

*

Children take what they assume
Is their own direction
Toward a character
They hope to achieve in maturity—
By adulthood it is too late—
Grandparents are important—
Children have to be able to compare
Unconsciously
The stages of life that each parent endures
With the stages they reach—
With only a parent they can't make that comparison—
They can't see the likely virtues and mistakes
Of adult life—
It is only in the couple generations
That patterns, life choices make a difference—
Children have little choice
But to emulate their accumulated parents
The likely source
Of all the choices they make—

*

If parents were as alert and responsive

To all children
As they try briefly to be with their own toddlers
What an extraordinary world this would be!

*

When childhoods are disrupted
Their adulthoods rarely are peaceful—

*

BEWARE THE MAN WHO REJECTS HIS FATHER

*

A baby is born with wisdom—
By the time he dies
He retains a mere echo of it—

*

We are given one song
In this life— .
How sweet and pure it is—
We take it up again
On the other side—

*

Children are the original geniuses—
But society imposes
Its own strictures and habits on them
Only a few rebel
Or retain some small independence—

*

Children learn rebellion at an early age
From parents who are blind to
Letting them be
Who they are compelled to be—

*

Can we blame an uncounseled child
For the trauma
That visits and corrupts his adulthood?

*

We treat our children like blotting paper—
We imprint them with our image
Which understandably and frequently
Comes out in reverse—

*

Whichever side of the mountain

We grow up on
Some of our memories
Are on the other side—

*

What might come from wretchedness
Might be a rare unexpected "Grosse Fuge"
An enduring symphony
A profound quartet
A certain result
A casual result
The vile result
An unintended result--

In a world engrossed in growing
complexity
Even a rare Grosse Fuge proves
unexceptional--
Even so, exceptional remains a likely
happening--
Only one person will have had
The history, and the vigor to write it--
No one else could have written it--
Simple fact--
But it was written—
We can say, fatuously
That we know suffering from him
And his Mt. Everest of a "Grosse Fuge"—

It might not have been written--
One remotely like it might have been written
Hundreds of times by a suffering world
And lost—
Our later version of it
Totally different but related
Might still be waiting to be written—
At present we consider whatever we call it
A likely possibility—
We wouldn't consider it
Even a far off phenomenon—

The price for the first has been paid—
No one can pay anything like
That price for its facsimile—
The time for that one Grosse Fuge has passed—
The world is buffeted now
By 100 year storms and calamities--
Heady results still come from suffering—
We thank those artists for having been hurt
And endured—
With less than contrition
We accept the good born out of the bad
And ignore its heavy cost--
Beat us, curse us, all of us, and the few
Who still must know the trial of suffering--
Let the few creators continue to suffer
So that we the less damaged

Can take heart from their gifts—

*

Thank god, we say silently
That Beethoven was battered and broken
Just enough to help him write
Heroic symphonies and pastorals—
If he had lived a Dumbledorean life
He'd have written the conventional—
If he had led our lives
He might not have written anything--

*

God, you sure know how
To turn a sow's ear into a silk purse—
You take the crummiest material
Kids blighted by alcoholic parents
Who have been subjected
To abuse, shame, indifferent educations
Who have had comforting souls stolen from them
And largely been cheated of survival skills
Then you turn this scum of the earth
Battered, defensive, loathsome
Into a world renown icon
Whom the world idolizes and loves—

There are so few of these miserable creatures!
We need more of them
So humanity can revel all the more in beauty—
Though the public chooses to look the other way
Certainly it should be rewarded
For working hand in hand with you, god
Adding more rigors if necessary
While you put on the finishing touches—
We need more geniuses—
In the exacting wisdom of your heart
Give us more of these execrable misfits—

*

We come to appreciate
All we've lost in life—
Pleasures echo at odd moments
When we need them—
They are gone
As well they should be—
We never say good bye to them—
They're gone—
And now
We're even more appreciative—

*

The humble man and the arrogant
Are they not always being themselves?
Who are their parents?
Where are their councilors?

*

The world owes us nothing—
To be sullen or bellicose
Is our own misjudged expression—
Neither parents or despots can be
blamed—
Personal responsibility is all—
It is to our advantage to use it—
However ill-prepared we are for life
Improvement is possible—
Our smallest adaptation
Can redefine our world—

*

The world conventionally accepts
That trial and tragedy create
Our original adventure and all the arts—
The world quietly acknowledges
That its prestige and pleasure
Is based on spent and broken lives—
Small price the world archly says
And then honors their achievements—
We cannot do less--

We hardly lighten the sufferers' plight—
Certainly we try, usually too late
With museums, shrines, and honors—
Small price—
But for every talent
That makes it through the traps
To produce reward for us
Uncountable hoards succeed in creating
Chaos and crime that counts for little
But tax expense and blight—

*

Our responsibilities belong to us—
Their final design is ours alone—

*

Martyrdom gets us martyrdom—
We need to give it up--

*

We are born into cultures
Near impossible to escape—
This is what our world is--
We think all of it is our own idea—

*

Whether we're about to trim a beard
Or build a cloud touching tower
These conditions had been forming
The outcome was being scheduled--

*

BIOGRAPHY IS SELF-ADULATION

*

Must a biographer
When he writes of an artist
Be an artist?

*

Biography is a statement
By the Delphic Oracle—
Interpretation is not without peril--

*

Unless a poet write it
The biography of an artist is dross—
Biographies provide the same macabre rewards
As a piano arrangement of a symphony—

*

Take the life of any artist
And follow it everywhere—
From birth and family
From conflict and early doubt
Listen, watch, hear and see
Whatever he's done
Wherever he's been--
Live his life, understand his conflict
His success, his temptations, his succumbing
Triumphs,
They've not always been called that—
His survival—
Endure as much of his drudgery and escapes
As you can—
"But that would be called a marriage!
He might as well be my spouse"—
Exactly--

*

Biography is translation from life—
Translation captures a fleeting shadow—

*

Gods floating in the sky
Never seem to touch the ground—
Biographers tracking less than gods
Find evidence of footprints—
Beethoven was human after all--

*

Forget the result—
Beethoven's hard luck story
Never will rival
Another guy's hard luck story—

*

When dreaming of walking
In the shoes of someone famous
Dare anyone say
"That guy was so lucky"?

*

Listeners taking pleasure
In Beethoven's mystifying music
Can't help being shaped
By his astonishing biography—

*

THE TRAGEDY OF BEETHOVEN

See how biographers sway us
(We are such easy believers)--
Mordant distress is sensationalized
Beyond what any of us poor mortals
Could survive—

*

When was misogyny classified as
High moral character?
Biographers claim that
Beethoven was of high moral character
A quality immediately appearing
In his music after abstract scrutiny—
We can't know how secure
Beethoven's moral character was—
His striving perhaps is an achievement--
But music conveys message so poorly--
Critics have offered interpretations
Of all of Beethoven's symphonies—
No doubt he searched and attempted...
And he changed—
His music suggests that—
We are blessed
That his humane character
Searched as deeply as it did--
But it must be safe to say
We interpret his music

Differently than he would--
This doesn't discount our musical debt
It heightens our devotional good will--

*

When detractors get too bold
The hero's defenders are happy
To take lines out of context—

*

A book in progress
Follows daily events
Is left behind
In popular consensus
And becomes everyday news
To be lost in ambiguity--

*

What stellar personality
Justifies forty pages of biography
On a probable Immortal Beloved
And then wearies us with thirty more pages
Of a custody battle gone wrong?
Lurid yellow pages!
No reader should suffer such sensation!

*

He probably fantasized his bond
To the Immortal Beloved
For the rest of his life
Or we did—
Real to him perhaps
And we should sympathize with his pain—
But only romantics
Are caught up in his delusion—

*

Curious, isn't it?
That an almost certain misanthrope
Lays claim to an Immortal Beloved?
What are the odds it's true?
Those efforts provide the artful longing
That prove he's human--

*

An Immortal Beloved!
A week in bed with her
Probably would have been
More than enough for Beethoven--

*

Oh come now, do we need
Beethoven's recurrent
Hiccups and bad dreams?

Our indulgent times
Have enough of those—

*

Amazing, it's difficult to understood—
Like the few of us
Who reach a flattering prestige
And think they have power--
Powerful people are ordinary men—
Those poor deceived people
They put down their scepters
As fast as ordinary people
Put down their splayed limbs--

*

I have a name
I've built a Wonder of the World building
I have a theory, a word, a religion
That will last an eternity—
Amazing what comfort that gives me
In the cold cold ground--

*

Intelligence is always trying
To figure out the mess
Stupidity has gotten us into—
It seldom recognizes natural raw dumbness

And misses the problem to be solved—

*

All opinions are equal—
Who expresses them
Makes the difference--

*

The critic comes along
Or a composer like Beethoven himself
And introduces revolution--
The artist's understanding or intent
Is beyond the critic's knowing
Or the audience's appreciation—
Who reads him but academicians?

*

To write about art
Is to intellectualize it—
The less said the better--

*

The more popular praise an art produces
The more theory it can foster—
Criticism as often raises the critic's
intelligence

Beyond the artist's conception—

*

We begin to enjoy Beethoven
Not because of his musicianship
But because he's been made
A teaching tool—

*

Art appreciation—
As constricted by
What we are told
We should like—

*

The meaning an audience finds
Might be a depth performers achieve
That the artist had no concept of--

*

Sometimes
The concert
Isn't the music—

*

Wouldn't it be great
If the benefactor's taste
Were the same as ours—

*

Beethoven's luck was notes
That couldn't be tied to meaning—
Words are the fly in the ointment--

*

Beethoven relied on a reputation
So grand
That people were willing to listen
To his anything—

*

What greater reward!
Look what
Beethoven could do in his time—
He could go from a ponderous opera
To three string quartets
And survive—
If he were a composer today
He'd be writing blockbuster music
For the movies
And his reputation would be only as good
As his last success--

Do we marvel
That he wrote three overtures
To a wooden opera?
How far we've gone from there--
He had a passion for music
But not for people—

*

Another Beethoven Fifth
On the radio!
That, and Schubert's Ave Maria
The be-all-and-end-all of music!
Surely someone could have written
An abbreviated "Four Seasons--"

*

As awesome as the arts are
They finally prove wearisome—
Often it is because the most popular
Are played to hummability—
This does not make them the best—
Some outlast their spark of inspiration—
Many composers had to be
The highly skilled workers of their day—
They had to stay busy to earn their keep—

*

Honoring Beethoven at every concert
Means neglecting other composers—
Beethoven assaults as his praise swells—
He is a marketing disaster—

*

Being the esteemed artist
Means valued
Ahead of every other artist—

*

Beethoven
Should not, cannot win
Every contest—

*

We have an obligation
To go beyond Beethoven--

*

One mountain alone in its place
Is an improbability—
One Beethoven
Filling the horizon
Is an abhorrence!

*

People haven't changed—
Their perceptions shift
With music's every new beat—

*

Shakespeare's not enough!
Now they're writing noble nonsense
About Beethoven!
No one is safe!

*

God!
While they're finding more meaning
In every word in the bible
They're finding more meaning
In every chord in Beethoven—

*

Beethoven's ruin was
That his faults were expunged
Until they were scarcely remembered—
Friends, music publishers
Owners of concert halls and biographers
Were happy to comply—

*

Rant and rave on, critic!
For all your effort
The world takes note of his talents
And then continues
On its unhurried, uninvolved way—

*

Why are we so afraid
To confront critics today
Or those solidly from the past?
Why do they have the authority
To mold our acceptance?
We know that taste is changing—
That certain worlds are crumbling—
The establishment always is under siege—
We need not apologize—
That is the way of the world—

*

Is it anything other
Than intellectual blather
To describe music?
What cheek to describe
The abstract—

*

Art cut, dried, expanded, or explained
By another
No longer belongs to the artist
And hardly anyone else, for that matter—

*

Add enough weight
To a reputation
And eventually
It collapses—

*

Words
Take us farther
From explanation—

*

Justification digs our hole deeper—

*

We call someone great
When we have molded him
Into an acceptable image—

When we have molded someone
Sufficiently into our own image

We are allowed to call him great--

*

The depth artists achieve
Isn't just what they've created
It is also their virtues
Audiences can wish for—

*

We use our judgments of famous lives
For purpose and pattern for our own lives—
Getting down to our basics
Would serve us better—

*

Would we choose to have dinner
With a malcontent like Beethoven?
Would we flatter ourselves
That he would entertain us
With or without his music?

*

Writing classical music
Does not make a superior person
Or a spiritual person—
We can't think we'd want

To meet Beethoven on the street—

*

Dazzled by his musical arrogance
Critics safely separated by time
See Beethoven as their hero—
It's a dark day when they discover
Like the rest of us he has feet of clay—

*

Tracking critics
And echoing them
Does not make us
Qualified voices—

*

The music critic speaks
To the person who wants to know
What's beyond the music he hears—
Most listeners assume they've come
For the music—
Critics hardly expand the music—
They inflate the mechanics—

*

An artist's private expressions

May comfort him
But they may not please an audience—
As often they test the tolerance
Of even small audiences
Privy to his innermost thoughts--

*

Beethoven gets the credit he does
Because he's become the sun to us--
We are safe ignoring the light
From stars diminished with distance—

*

Beethoven didn't ruin music
But his admirers almost did—
They accepted esoteric music
Meant to be enjoyed
By the cognoscenti—

Yes, it's the composer's privilege
To write for whom he wants—
But we are free to question the results
Beyond his given reasons--

*

"Inexplicable art—"
"His art was inexplicable!"

Naïve?"
Simple?
Artless?
How do we come to defend art
Or realize it must be defended?
What art, ever, must be defended?
The outrageous?
A disrespectful icon?
The exceptional?
Is there such a thing?
Stripping an art of its importance?

Every art resides within the privacy
Of every individual—
No art is more worthy than its humanity—
Humaneness is an implied definition
Art fights for—

*

Being trail blazers isn't always an
achievement—
Sometimes they reach a destination
They didn't intend to visit--
Mostly they search, only hoping to arrive--
A Schubert may be more enjoyable, all in all
Than a Beethoven who has forged ahead
Alone—

*

Sometimes we have to bypass
The bridge in the future
That was to take us
Where we thought we must go—

*

To go forward
Beethoven tried to get beyond himself
And reclaim music
Already being lost to time—
When he got there
He had lost music—

*

Perhaps Beethoven's notebooks prove otherwise
But does much of his brave indomitable music
Show rage and frustration?
The composer doth protest too much—
All this bluster and fist shaking
Noble and arrogant—
We put up with that bombast because
Those virtues still have life—

*

Whatever its speculative worth
The spiritual development of a composer
Likely depends on the survival
Of his composition books—

*

It is not our job to figure out
How a composer worked out
A difficult piece—
It is our job
To find the music presented
Enjoyable—

*

A lot depends
On how fortuitously surprises fit together—
Luckily Beethoven didn't tap out
A Nazi anthem
Or he'd be in a public relations
Pickle!

*

Some think god took eons
To create simple life
And even more time
To create a slug or worm—
Variation

Losing one, gaining another—
We think we're the crowning glory
The first for being able
Or wanting to and needing to
Praise god
With such effort and sad purpose—
But a few of us
Not just theologians and musicians
Would say this is an intellectually
disciplined god
Who, working with next to nothing
Created a world of subtlety and sureness
In an advancing time
We finally could understand—
Like Beethoven did
Godlike, with nothing
Four notes, rhythm and variation—

Do you believe him
When the world's most intelligent man says
"There is a god"?
It's too bizarre
Calling intellectual creation
Steps toward art—
Puzzle solving?
Creation was a decorative trinket
Of leisure
Until Adam and Eve--
And then, end of suspense--
We got into the act—

God could have written that story
A lot sooner—
And Beethoven, the god of music!
The world waiting for him
Unable to go on without him!
We think highly enough of him already—

*

MUSIC WITHOUT THEORY

It was Beethoven's role to figure out
How to put four notes together
Composing a symphony—
How he did it isn't our concern—
Our expectation is to enjoy the work—
If his solution works
So much the better—
But solutions are not
The style and be all of music—
Artists revise until their efforts attract
A public response—

*

While we can be empathetic
We are unable to suffer another's
Even a composer's pain—
And if he can't get beyond it
In his music

We can't suffer his music either—

*

The depth artists achieve is meaning
Most audiences have been encouraged to find—

*

The absurdity—
Partisan experts give us music insights
Into a man who fluffed his first steps
Toward a good life—

*

Glory and Value go together
"Like a Horse and Carriage—"
Give me credit for finding a current image—
If we could stop glorifying Beethoven
We might hear something different
In his music—

*

We hold artists up as intellectual superlatives
And then wonder why

They don't have emotional merit—

*

Criticism is for grave stones—

*

Poor old Charlie
Up against old Beethoven!
Doesn't he know
He hasn't a chance!
But he has as much right
To be wrong as anybody else—

*

There it is:
A hundred years of rejecting
Beethoven's divine opus numbers—
It's like a dam bursting—

*

Surely I can be excused
If I attempt to wobble
Beethoven's pedestal a bit—

*

First I took on god—
Then it was Beethoven—
Next will be Motherhood—

*

Anyone taking interest
In these Beethoven rants
Would say they speak more
About the ranter
Than about Beethoven—

*

Who, but someone unlearned
In composition is justified
To expose his disappointment
In Beethoven the complexicrat?

*

In a life, much of love and beneficence
It looks like my malice and bad humor
Is directed at Beethoven—
Life's quirks are hard to explain—
His reputation, interfering
With music and pleasure for me
Pushes me down a thorny path—

*

When I cut cross-grain
Against bits and pieces
Of all that is wholesome
Christ of love
Beethoven's defiance and bravery
It's difficult to find justification—
The world is so fully invested
In invented sentiments
I'm throwing darts
Against a stone wall—

*

When I want to be obnoxious
It comes easily
I ask: What would Beethoven do?

*

While mixing a martini—
Beethoven in the other room--
Screw Beethoven—

*

It is not Beethoven I find so horrific—
It is our efforts to create
A misaligned heroism—
We magnify his suffering

Make it a fateful vendetta
Only he was able to surmount—
We surfeit on his heroism—
Beethoven suffered
And he conquered it in music—
For us that's all that matters—

Beethoven suffered--
Eluding love
He was conquered by suffering—

*

Heroic!
I wish I had a penny
For every time "heroic" was used—
I'd be a millionaire—

*

Nobody ever said
Beethoven was writing for me—
He must have thought
He was sacrificing himself
For his music—
He thought vindication would come to him
But he was wrong about the reason--
Maybe I don't cotton to him—
That's not his choice, it's mine--

*

No need to talk about Beethoven
And the heights—
I try to bring him down to earth!
Beethoven could also be
The Carlsbad Cavern of music—

*

It is his reputation, first as a composer
And secondly as a person
That is my contention--
Beethoven is a most misunderstood man—
Man, composer?
How thoroughly they get entangled—

*

It is possible, even desirable
To put Beethoven in perspective
We whores, buying at the lowest bid?
He is not a singular landscape—
If we gauge men
By their money, art, intellectual value
Beethoven is not the one path to the
stars—
He is part of a broad highway
Crowded with many travelers
Who have made the way smooth

By their tread—

*

We forgive ugly lives
For the great gifts they give us—
We look for the best price
Whores that we are—
Distance diminishes our qualms
About the price—

*

We interpret his life
As exemplary as we can--
Beethoven had so much respect for himself
That he was able to push us
As far as he wanted to go—

*

If we don't want to be
Proven wrong
We must talk only to ourselves—

*

Beethoven thought so well of himself
That his personality was a strong part
Of his music—

Lots of bluster, lots of "I'll show them
How daring and original music can be--"
Some charm and humor too
He was human after all
A walk in the woods in the Sixth
A search for a lost penny
But his final view of himself
Was to tell us how fearless he was
Toward his exaggerated view
Of a world's opposition--

*

We dare not call it
The Law of Compensation
But Beethoven was so lucky
With the imperative
To be a serious composer
That he was virtually excluded
From being a warm acceptable
Human being—

*

Beethoven got screwed
By his own proficiency—
Youthful prowess
Allowed him to compose
His popular pieces—
His growing technical fitness

His reputation
His growing arrogance
Led him astray in his maturity—
Partisans support his late pieces
Because they imply intellectual progress—

*

Beethoven's heart was lost to his music—
He showed comic relief here and there—
No one completely abandons social
conduct
(I couldn't be that stone hearted)
But straining to master music
He evaded humanity—
As he suffered poverty of heart
His music suffered the loss—
How much differently he might have
written—

*

Power and piss
Thunder and lightning
All heads-up and forward—
He did have his soft moments—
But this is the picture
This man who cannot find peace
Parenthetically presents—

*

Bluster
Composers agree--
Beethoven—

*

Essentially
Beethoven was a blowhard
Who took himself
Seriously—

*

Oh yes, genius!
It must defend itself
Against enemies
It creates—

*

Art is not martyrdom—
Benefiting life
Is the purpose of art—
However well meaning
Art for a cause approaches
Unsubstantial intelligence—

*

The mind reveals
Even the little it has recollection of--
The mind can't hide--
It is compelled to applaud itself
At every available opportunity--

*

Why would an artist bad-mouth
His audience!
Beethoven undoubtedly played
Before society's most sophisticated
audiences—
They read music, played instruments
Composed
And avidly attended concerts—
If Beethoven was so advanced, so confusing
Is that their fault?
Or biography's?

*

What artist would be so boorish
As to disparage
His audience's incomprehension?

*

A Master

Who trivializes our talents
Is a tyrant—

*

Martyrdom begets martyrdom—
We need to give it up--

*

We forget
That mechanics and passion
Are two different things
When talking about music's effects
On us--

*

Rapport seldom comes from intelligence—
Rapport comes from heart
Which is the world's soft stability—

*

Some creations are so virtuoso
They lose the claim of art—
Their ideas are so clever
They are lost
To thought's next breeze—

*

Unfortunately for us
The definition of art
Has become so diffuse
High and low
That it is meaningless--

*

The intellect Beethoven transmuted
To passion became anger—

*

Much of Beethoven's life
Seems colored by anger—
That's hardly a solid base
For public acceptance—

*

Proving superiority
Is a hopeless task—
Isn't there another goal?
Pastimes that give
Immediate pleasure?

*

I would rather hear
Shakespeare humming
Than Beethoven strumming
New chords—

*

Listen!
Beethoven
Isn't wearing
Any music!

*

Well, you have to admit
Beethoven had curiosity
And intellectual energy—
Luckily he overcame the use of them
Some of the time—

*

Have we ever been meant
To have all the answers?
Isn't it more likely
We should have
As many questions as possible?

*

We hardly can be held accountable
For the lives we were given
But we can try to reconcile them
To the Great Equalizer in the sky—

*

Let's hear it for good ol' Ludwig!
Three cheers for Beethoven!
His Ninth has a brave beerhall bounce--

*

Three cheers for Beethoven!
Reaching, attempting—
So important to him
But often a disappointing dead end
For us—

*

It's Beethoven again!
He had little tolerance for human complexity—
Isn't that what moral regard is?

*

The composer is most free
Of all the artists—

Oh to soar like a bird!
But no gift is without its cost—

*

Does the composer hear the music
Before he writes it down?
He must always hear it first—
That is the only way he can know it is true—

*

Obviously it's difficult to contradict scholars
Who have charted every note Beethoven wrote—
But if he first didn't write down his works
From inner harmony and joy, from intuition
Where his music was going
He was no artist
But merely a technician—
Of course there are revisions
And sudden and difficult insights
That give the scholars
Their breathless discoveries—
These complexities exist—
But if these creations aren't in the man first
As infinite beauty and joy

He and the world are wrong
In calling him an artist—
Creativity is only part
Of what man is--

*

All his compositional labor
Should tell us something—
Why all those tiresome chords
Endlessly plunking—
They are nothing to us—

*

If "deep" is meant to capture
The essence of boring
Beethoven certainly achieved the heights—

*

To kill us with exhaustion
Was that Beethoven's purpose
With his "Hammerclavier"?
With that he almost lost
The title artist—

*

The "Hammerclavier" is a dead tree

Standing tall
In a green forest—

*

Any artist who is consciously trying
To exhibit his deepest emotions
Is morbid—
An artist's role is to entertain—
He can bring his audience to deep waters
But holding their heads under
Is not part of the bargain—

*

If we're going to give names
To compositions
Beethoven's "Hammerclavier"
Should be called
"The Never Ending"
"The Murky"
"The Obsessive"
"The Morbid"--
I need not go on—

*

What does it come down to?
Ravel's piano concertos
Against Beethoven's?

Rachmaninoff against
Beethoven's symphonies?
Who cares how long
They were in preparation
Or how many themes
They collected in notebooks?
Time vs heart?
The desire is to get along
As best one is able—

*

Intellectualism
Is routine—
Inspiration
Is capturing the infinite—

*

Intellectual challenge
Jumping through hoops
Toeing the mark--
Some art intrigues
But art should be spontaneous and natural
Coming seemingly from the artist
As effortlessly as it is received by the audience—

*

Try not to compose and color
With thirty different instruments—
Try to be free
Dip, glide, fly
By the wind's dictation—
Akin to nature's impulse
Free to be
Free to create--

*

Beethoven is a great composer
Because dumb events buffeted him
And pushed him in a direction—
Pushing was part of his chemistry--
Pushing back made a difference—

*

THE AGE OF PERMANENCE IS OVER

*

The Heroic Age is over—
Enough of heroes grabbing the prize
Enough of vanquishing the meek
Of cursing the gods
Of claiming mastery and glory—
The Heroic Age was
The Age of Ignorance

The Age of Tragic Presumption
The Age of Drastic Inequality—
Dawning enlightenment
Made heroism suspect
And close to obsolete—

We're going to hell
In a smart phone
Because of heroism--

*

The terrible truth is
We seldom establish peace
Through victory—

The terrible truth is
Fairness can be achieved
Without conflict--

*

No man should feel shamed
Or embarrassed
But it's hardly an honor
To be called a god--

*

Except for the prize

Few composers would want to go
Where Beethoven went
The Valley of Worn-out Fighters!

*

Beethoven's heights are solid--
We climb them
Under our own power--

*

Anger appeared to be the power
That Beethoven used to control
His snapping patrons--
But it was his art that kept him safe—

*

Years make it easier to accept
Beethoven's wretched character—
Except for the pathos of deafness
The poor man himself is forgotten—
In time art ends up as art
Without an artist--

*

We accept arrogance
Because of its sometimes valuable rewards—

Harmful effects are less measurable—

*

Beethoven was directed by his deafness—
Ego drove him to search deeper—
He didn't care if we followed him or not—
We value arrogance
When it promises great rewards—

*

Poor old Beethoven—
He forgot he was writing music
And forged a weapon
For fighting life—
Poor old man
He couldn't accept that his gift
Hard fought for
Was to reconcile him to life—

*

Art, however long or short
However strong or weak
Whatever its competition
Works for a measure of serenity—

*

Lucky for us, we say after the fact
Beethoven's pride as composer
Was stronger than his willingness
To cry, beg, or retreat—
In spite of his pride
He even deserves sympathy--

*

When most of his enemies were gone
Beethoven won respect
For what his intelligence provided:
The limits of music—

*

Emotions are so volatile
They can be induced
With sub-particle flashpoints—
But the long roiling repetition of them
Seduces original artists to think
These tactics are normal—

*

His agitation advanced
Beyond the age of measured art
As his character slipped into outrage—

*

The tragedy of Beethoven's last music is
That he left his heart and ours
Out of it—

*

Beethoven's devil demanded
Much more—
Popular acceptance
Had to be given up—

*

Was it ego?
Beethoven finally didn't concern himself
With music of the day—
He had to write what stormed within him—

*

We have our choice of stereotypes—
The people who let things go
Are matched
By the people who strive too much—
Being driven has its limits—
Enjoying things as they are
Live as let live suggests
A compatible goal—

*

As smoothly as honey
Up-righted in a bottle
Seeks a level
At bottom from top
As beautifully as a knot shapes itself
Into a bow
As quietly as a postman delivers
To our mail box dependably
So can the world bring sequence
To your life—

*

"What if I gave you
All my operas, symphonies, and sonatas?"
"What if I gave you all 1001 pages of my poems?"
"What if I gave you a Wall around China
Of my paintings?"
"If you had given me all of that
Would you have given me anything?
Would you have given me yourself?
Shouldn't that have been the contribution?"

*

Yes, I willingly endure any pain
So my abusive lover can paint another masterpiece
Or, likely a mediocre blob—

How am I to know?
Yes, I will live through any degradation
So my brother can rape me
And provide another passionate score—
Yes, I will submit to my uncle's vicious cruelty—
I'm happy to be of no account
So a criminal can give his gifts to the world
And win honor and fame for himself—

*

My canvases on the wall
My images on a screen
My music filling an auditorium
Ever enriching the economy--
What does it matter
If none of my efforts
Lead toward peace?

*

Artists, those who bother at all
Tend to justify their production
As payment for ill begotten lives—

Artists are the servants we all are--
We don't need uppity artists—

*

Should we excuse the artist
For art being his only consideration
And not care if he was a good man?
In the real world this never is the case—
Everyone's first concern ought to be
To be a good person—
If it is only creative work that is applauded
We are encouraging social misery—
Crassness decides our willingness
To pay that price—
We all should be able to accept
That this is not a price
We want to pay—

*

We all earn wages
For who we are and who we are not—
We pray that bonuses outweigh the fines—
For most of us they're fairly balanced—
It is only our jealous minds
That think some are grossly rewarded—

*

We have to identify with others—
We are not human
Until we can bond one with another—
Living alone is not a happy choice—

Whatever we do creatively
Whoever we justify doing it for
If we do not have love for others
For as many as we can fit into our lives
We are lone, abject failures--
As there is no one who matters in our lives
We must always know
That we matter little to anyone—

*

Poet or architect
Farmer or financier
Fakir or fumbler
Our gifts
Do not entitle us to any more
Than what any other person deserves—
We are all worthy
We are all equal—
The equality is love—

*

Without the search it is not possible
For everyone to live with an artist—
But sit across from one
And watch him work—
What satisfaction!
And if everyone fulfills himself

As an artist
What better person to sit across from!

*

Notice--
I was one of the friends
Who recognized, but couldn't define
The accomplishment of this artist--
I stayed with him not on aesthetics
But on friendship—

*

No one lives up to
All he advocates or wants to live—
Maybe Jesus came close—
It's a shame he couldn't live longer
As a man—

*

We are always writing of a god
We know nothing about—

*

FAITH IS EXCLUSIVE OF INTELLIGENCE

*

We spend so much time
With concepts of god
Without admitting
He might be there—
That's the way
With enduring relationships—

*

All the intelligence in the world
Has no more weight
Than the lightest brain in the world
In proclaiming an existence of god—

*

Better to be a genius
And live in a miserable world?
Better to be a nobody
And enjoy a benevolent world?
Better to be grateful
In the creation of a loving world--

*

Civilization's goal
Is to fashion love
As the stable condition
Of life—

The best of civilized life
Begins and ends with
"I love you--"

*

Love, so pervasive
One in want of love
Can write of love—

*

The goal is spontaneous harmony—
Whatever doesn't lead to it
Is erroneous thought or action--

*

Worldly ambitions
Art, philosophy, children
None of them is justification
For not living a good life—

*

We give ordinary men little credit
For their accomplishments
We do not comprehend—
Our appreciation should be as great

For everyone, and artists, great and small—

*

From the inmost chamber of his heart
The composer is most able
Of all the artists
To create worlds outside himself—

*

Music is the most fragile of the arts—
So often it must be wedded with words
To keep it faithfully in the heart—

*

How does an artist confirm
That what is in his heart
Is good?
It is axiomatic
That heart is the source of good—

*

ODE TO JOY

We are rewarded as fully
As any saint or holy man—
In possessions, lusts, and pleasures

We are as rich as any man
Of enlightenment—
We are bound, we are buoyed
In ever present love—
No one can do better than that—

*

Which came first
Melody or heart?

Which came first
The title
Or the music?

*

We expect it--
Don't we deserve
To be praised
For what we do best?

*

Melody is heart--
Heart is the loving part
Of a person's being--

*

Pain can elicit heart—
But if pain turns to anger
Heart can be lost
And song and story are lost
And art is lost—

*

Sometimes practical comes close
To heart—
But nothing is a substitute
For heart—

*

Creation springs
From the heart
Flows
Through the head
To the void beyond
And begins
The cycle
Anew—

*

The eyes are an appendant organ—
The heart is primary for seeing—

*

What our senses don't comprehend
Our hearts bring into accord—

*

Music hath charms
That knows nothing
Of knowing--

*

A score textured
To ensnare the subconscious
Seldom has the beauty
To move the heart—

*

To be short of benevolence
Is not to be fully human—

*

No heartier or more grateful
A "Thank you"
Than for a door
Held open for you—

*

Yes, we should attempt to share
The pain of others—
But the unstinting pain of others grows thin—
We sense that some of it is caused
Less from outside than inside--
We might wish that pain subsides
With spiritual growth—

*

Nothing is free—
Happiness is not free—
If you're quick
Art comes closest
To being a gift--

*

We all deserve better from people
Than we receive—
We all owe more to people
Than we give—
This in no way equalizes our relationships—
It means
That love is ever so much more critical
In our lives—

*

The lord loves a gracious giver—
If our gift can't be gracious
Well, we can postpone our gift—
The key word is "gracious—"
The gift is to be ours—
If we can't give it
Graciously
We haven't discovered the reason
For giving—

*

It is giving itself
That is the gift—

*

WE ALL HAVE GIFTS

*

The wonder of Nature is
That it creates
Every unmatchable one of us—
Me, you, us, them
Beethoven—

*

I am a surprise to me—
You are a surprise to you—

Come, let us astonish each other—

*

We facilitate miracles
By making life a joy--

*

We are free
We are beautiful
We are meant to lift the world—

*

Every person we meet is
A fountain, a sprinkler, or a geyser—
We can drink or go thirsty—
We can drink at bright splashing places
We can slurp from cool shady pools
We can splash together barefooted
We can walk or dance refreshed
In renewed confidence—

*

Maybe the egoless create
The great art
Effortlessly—
Whatever godhood is

It is egoless and effortless—

*

Joy is religion
Joy is god—

*

Any creator
Who expands our amiability
Deserves our gratitude and respect—
The whole point to art may be
To strengthen our creation of joy—

*

If the everyday workings of our minds
Don't bring us joy
Why do we value their efforts?

*

Enjoying the arts
For the pleasure they give us
Instead of what they are purported to be
Surely is the primary joy—

*

CREATION IS JOY

*

Creation completed
Brings joy—
It is reflected
In a universe wide creation—
Oh joy!

*

Through formalizing, joy is lost—
We smother it with law
With calendar and preparation—
Joy joy joy—
We do not destroy it
We do not rediscover it
We do not re-invent it—
It always is there—
We need but latch on to it--

*

Life is too glorious!
We do not earn it
We do not wangle or steal it--
Make sure we deserve it—

*

Some of us were separated at birth
From illustrious siblings
And have lived apart all our lives—
We sense a truth in that—
But the older we get
Those of us so fortunate believe
We have been together all our lives
And belong together
And are destined to be together
All our lives, forever
The repetition confirming—

*

If we're an artist
Can we not know
Our creation is waiting
In jeopardy in the next blink?
If we're a parent
Can we not know
Our child is hungering
For love and guidance?
If we're a person of this world
Can we not know
That the smallest and the largest
Is dependent on our care and good will?

*

Too much is lost
Between word and deed--

*

We sing our joy to the world--
What difference if the song be
Short and cracked
Mixed in mood and clarity?
What if it is sung so many times
It seems a stirring part of the air?
What if unheard beyond our smile
Or forgotten by day's close?
We sing our joy--
It is our gift to the world
It is the world's gift to us--

*

Is he joyous?
So many questions
Answer themselves—

*

In unqualified ways
We conduct original lives
That never earn the title genius--
When everyone is called a genius
In his humble individual way

We are not being sarcastic or
embellishing—
We are stating fact—
Creation is a joyous calling—
If it is not received as the sunshine of life
It is not creation—
If it is hidden connections
Dull mind in bleakness
It is harried and willful--
And then there's Beethoven
To be driven!

All that suffering hyperbole!
Thank a generous god
That some of his work must have
given him
Joy—
That poor tormented man—
Who conquered music like a demon!
His sick old life had little pleasure—
He had to master, rule, conquer—

If that is what creation is
Volcanoes are still competing
With dinosaurs for mastery--

*

Labor squeezes the joy
Out of art—

*

Whatever our circumstances
Our best guarantee of inner peace
Is our satisfaction in ourselves—

*

Art not of the heart
Is harrowing existence
Is work—

If it is not composed
From within our unlearned hearts
It will never be art—

*

How much intense labor
Must go into
Ending a symphony?
Is it a search for perfection
Or an exaggerated need
To overcome doubt?

*

We acknowledge a Mt. Everest
The Shakespeare, Marconi, Darwin—

The subtler sciences include
All the extraordinary accomplishments--
They are recognized
As nodes studding a continent—

*

We owe humanity to everyone—
Being great, in any field
Doesn't suspend our responsibility—
If we aren't of humane stature
What merit is genius?
Honor hardly is warranted
For our succeeding where we can—

Being an incomplete person
Has never meant we can't be great
artists—
As much as we prize the heroic
It means our influence is much narrower—

*

Mockingbird, what makes us equal?
The fact that you're so small
And short lived
And that I'm hobbling about
On a painful knee?
What are the facts of equality?
There are none—

Love... do not say the word
Stretches gossamerlike, steel beamlike
Across all time and space...
Do not mention those either—

*

We are a vast field in bloom—
Our creativity presses each other—
We support and climb and tumble
Over each other—
What is the season?
What is the clime?
We are of this generation
And we disappear with it--

*

The artist sits
At one end of the teeter-totter—
A benefactors sits
On the other end—
Do they balance?
Do they kick off in harmony?
Do they rise and fall together?
Is there a need to trade places?

*

Equality is impossible

In every instance—
But personal satisfaction
Creates a genuine equality
That cannot be undone—

*

Equality certainly
Is not an achievable social goal—
But a person's satisfaction with himself
Is a quality that is truly harmonious—
Satisfaction ratifies all rank, privilege, wealth—
Any comparisons are of no driving concern—
Edges are smoothed over in a way
That dissatisfaction can never spoil--

*

Unless we treat everyone as equals
We will make little progress
In accepting people—
We who hardly are artists
Great statesmen or entrepreneurs
Until we give up sycophancy
We will not dare say we have merit—

*

Our sycophancy
Is a brake
On our genius—

*

We have to invest with others—
We are not human
Until we can discard comparisons
And identify one with another—
Other has no substitute—
We cannot live happily alone—
Whatever we do creatively
Whoever we justify doing it for
If we do not have love for others
For as many as we can fit into our lives
We are alone--
We are abject failures if we ask
The quiet question
"Is there anyone who matters in my life?"
And the answer is "no—"

*

We owe everyone our humanity
While his respect for us is our due—
Applause in one field
Doesn't excuse deficiencies in another—

*

The demand of burgeoning art
Is that we are obliged to be better
people—

*

We want to have a good life—
Maybe it won't quite be bursting with love
And accomplishment—
But of the few people we come into contact
with
We would like them to be able to say
As we would want to say
"He was a good person—"

*

Contemporary fame means nothing—
Famous people are forgotten
As quickly as ordinary people
Unless it is, and it is only
Their work continuing to influence
The future—

*

WHAT IF WE ARE HERE FOR A REASON

*

Our first duty
Is not to be
A totally acceptable person
But to be a good person—
Everything follows from that—

*

Fabulous and famous people
Rich people and powerful
Doers and shakers are people,
Little different from us—

*

Wealth is the only thing
That has a little effect on time—
But all the money in the world
Is impounded by time's collapse—

*

The artist's art creates the artist's life—
The artist is what he creates—
And then the art—
True for everyone?
Who are you?
What are you?
The creator of your own life—

The artist has no one
To address his message to
But the people of his time—
Who else could he possibly give voice to?
His ideas might be more nuance
And therefore something strange
But who would admit
Something is beyond his power
To understand?
He has no alternative
At any time—
He is a prisoner of his now—

*

That ungrateful soul, Beethoven
When dying raised his fist to the sky—
What did he have to complain about!
He could have laid his hands
Across his chest
In those final moments
And tried to be grateful
While drawing those last few breaths—

*

Just questioning—
Beethoven intuited immortality
And he shook his fist?

*

Are we to believe
Beethoven actually shook his fist
When dying?
It seems so much in character--
At whose say so?
What a terrible thing certainty—
What a horrible thing, judgment—

*

How can we call ourselves happy
If our fear of unhappiness follows?
We reach the place where
Happiness and unhappiness are one
Where we accept both
As the due order of things
Without gradation or shade
Neither deserved or undeserved—

*

We enter a period of refinement—
That is a way of preparing for death--

*

THE MEANING OF CHAPEL

I've not been a Rothko fan—
I fail to see profundity
In a canvas of two or three shades
Subtly merging—
But I draw hope from a Rothko Chapel
A room of like canvases—
Dark purples, maroons, black
Lit by the same light in his studio—
I find courage—
But Rothko committed suicide
Months before finishing this work—
Is a man an artist
When he cannot be sustained
By a project of such anticipated impact?
Where is art's strength and encouragement
If the artist himself cannot find solace
In his own near finished work?
I bear a grief that
Even with such a grand concept
bolstering him
His life of art could not sustain him—
A weight of sorrow
That art itself cannot alleviate—
What fights, what doubts, what tragedy
loomed
When his chapel, as calm and assuring
As he had reason to accept
Could not protect him?

*

Have you noticed
How many people are dying?

*

Dying itself is not all that serious—
It depends on your point of view--
Thank god we must die—
But how we die matters—
Torturously, too late
Unexpectedly, after much distress—
Timely, with grace and humor—
Death is a congenial host—
We should accept its invitation
accordingly—

*

How many proposals
For death do we need
To die peacefully?

*

Lament is short lived—
Deny all we want
Artists and wise men die
Their works also in time—

*

The closer we are to the long end
The closer we are to the faceless
beginning—

*

How many volumes have been written
On the ideal way to die?
Don't bother listing them—
I have found the way:
While reading the comics—
You don't understand?
Light hearted and exhaling laughter
(It's all relative)
Going out and up
Reading the comics—

*

You know how arbitrary life is
When a fond humorist has to die—

*

If I could be near as funny
As the comedians
Of this upside down world

I couldn't be a happier man—

*

I would be happy
If my sense of humor
Were the last to go—
A last laugh
Not as cynical acknowledgement
Of a false and hollow world
But an easy spontaneous laugh
For the sheer joy of it—

*

A good way to die?
with a smile on my face—
A better way to die?
With music
In my heart—
The best way to die—
Love embracing--

*

The purple finch's answer:
"If I could tell you why we die
I could not sing—"

Do not take this personally—

Neither I or a cat that kills
Take my death personally—
Do not take this poem personally—
We live in a world too large
For "personally—"
We are too anonymous
To be "personally"—

*

Skulls are staring at me—
They are so stupid!
Or does their silence
Make them wise?
I'd like to detect a smile
But their eyes have sunk
To darkness—
I sense no message—
Stupid skulls—

*

The names recorded in my address book
Faded, and some in fresh black ink
Grow more irrelevant every day—

*

In life everything comes with edge—
Only death is without edge—

It is called eternity—

*

Death finally means
Freely letting go--

*

Rain falls
On me and a dead tree--
We are blessed—

A falling leaf touches my hand—
Blessings come from everywhere—

*

In the space
Of one of my brain cells dying
A green leaf sprouts—

*

Keep growing, little tree--
You are taking my place—

*

We are takers—

We give back so little—
I write
Less and less—
Old age makes me feel useless—
Old age makes it imperative
That I contribute—
I give all, I give so much
In that final little letting go—
Going out balances coming in—

*

Constricted when free
Free while oppressed—
Enduring reversals
Is rolling with life--

*

Approaching death is a waste of time
If it doesn't bring us closer to love--

*

We must let the world go—
We are responsible for ourselves
Until we can't help ourselves—
Pain ends—
If it doesn't
Joy is compensation—

Life is short—
Pain?
We avoid it
As much as we can—
And if we can't
We're a short time here—

*

Blessing and rewards—
Blessings and punishment—
Life is happenstance—
Justification doesn't gilt edge life
And should disappear with age—
Death comes naturally—

*

Cliché will have to do—
Lightning is prone to strike
Mountain tops—

*

Imagine, a person
Poorly fitting the description
Of a human being--
A Beethoven
Being a revered composer—

*

When you get beyond
The blustery bellicose Beethoven
Pathetic isn't he
You get to an inner man
Alone, frightened
And much in need of comfort—

*

He's an oddly shaped
Good person—
Brusque and rude
Impertinent and off putting—
But he has a sense
Of honor, duty
An insecure sense of love—
He wants to do the right thing
But he's short with people—
An oddly shaped good person—
My god, that's Beethoven!
Maybe he's not
No one is
The greatest composer in the world
But he's a man for all that
And he does deserve love—

*

Listen to what you write about love—
Listen to what Beethoven writes—
Listen to what you write about music—
How can you not love Beethoven?

*

Beethoven, you're an ass!
Also a person!
No other reason
To love you—

*

At last
The giant becomes
A man—

*

We follow
Reluctantly—
We wish we wouldn't
But he draws us
Ineluctably deeper—
Beethoven--

*

Why Beethoven?

Because he is there—

*

ES MUSS SEIN
It must be—

*****

The names of fools appear everywhere--

ABOUT THE AUTHOR

Charles Whistler moved to Florida as a young man and, on his way, discovered Zen, haiku poetry, and the moon. These were his beginning tools as an author. Writing seriously, humorously, exaltedly, and divisively about god gave him reason to leave a broader trail.

Growing confidence and dedication to his craft have allowed him to produce volumes of work. Reading and writing steadily, revising, being work shopped, and judged by qualified critics have sharpened his skills. Obviously commercial and scholastic successes are a truer standard and the only guarantee of relevance and worth. But credentials and reputation, finally, are for readers to define. His philosophy can be summed up as follows:

> Inspiration is a leaf
> Erratic in drift—
> But like the arctic tern
> That flies from pole to pole
> The poet must be
> Ever vigilant and without rest—
> Inspiration must be sustained
> By direction and dedication—`

Printed in the United States
By Bookmasters